❧❧❧❧❧❧❧❧❧❧❧❧❧❧❧❧❧❧❧❧❧❧

Cindy heard Ashley shriek, "Grant, no! Don't you dare! It was an accident. Honest!" Laughing and giggling, she came tearing around the corner of the house and nearly collided with Cindy. She stopped and stared at her. "Oh, Cindy! What are you doing here?"

Cindy looked behind Ashley and saw Grant, soaking wet in his shorts and a polo shirt.

"Um, Grant just stopped by to . . . well, we're working on a surprise for you," Ashley continued.

"Well, I'm surprised," Cindy said, forcing a smile.

"Hey, Cindy, I know this looks funny," Grant said. "But I wasn't in the pool." Cindy looked at him incredulously. "I mean, I was in the pool, but that wasn't what I came over for."

"Isn't that nice," Cindy said with control. "Well, I'll let you guys get back to work."

She turned away and headed for her bike, tears stinging her eyes as she climbed on and rode toward home.

❧❧❧❧❧❧❧❧❧❧❧❧❧❧❧❧❧❧❧❧❧

FAWCETT GIRLS ONLY BOOKS

SISTERS

THREE'S A CROWD #1

TOO LATE FOR LOVE #2

THE KISS #3

SECRETS AT SEVENTEEN #4

ALWAYS A PAIR #5

ON THIN ICE #6

STAR QUALITY #7

MAKING WAVES #8

SISTERS

MAKING WAVES

Jennifer Cole

FAWCETT GIRLS ONLY • NEW YORK

A Fawcett Girls Only Book
Published by Ballantine Books
Copyright © 1987 by Cloverdale Press, Inc.

Library of Congress Catalog Card Number: 86-91307

ISBN 0-449-13208-0

Manufactured in the United States of America

First Edition: February 1987

Chapter 1

*O*nly the top of Cindy Lewis's curly blond head was visible as she bent over her desk, rushing to do her geometry assignment before the teacher came in. As she turned her big green eyes toward the clock on the wall, she saw she had only five minutes to finish. With swim-team practice or meet after school every day, it seemed like she was always behind in her homework. Any free time she did have, she spent with Grant on the beach. She hated to waste her few free evening hours doing homework.

"Just as she finished the last problem, someone bumped her arm, causing her to draw a jagged arcline through it. Cindy looked up abruptly. She was about to snap, "Hey, watch it!" when she saw a petite dark-haired girl. Cindy noticed the girl's trembling lower lip and the frightened look on her face.

"I'm sorry. I hope I didn't ruin your paper."

"It's okay."

"Is this seat taken?" she asked, pointing to the chair behind Cindy.

"Not yet. Sit down. Mrs. Kaufman is a nut about seating charts, though, so you may end up somewhere else. You must be new. I'm Cindy Lewis."

"Ashley Corbett. My dad got transferred, so we just moved here from Oregon. I wanted to finish out the school year there, but my parents wanted to get settled here as soon as possible."

Ashley set her books down and sat in the desk behind Cindy. Her curly dark hair fell into her face as she leaned forward to set her purse on the floor beside here. Cindy turned back around to clean up her paper.

Mrs. Kaufman entered the room just before the bell rang. She wore one of her standard tan skirts with matching orthopedic shoes. She was an older teacher with a well-earned reputation for being tough but fair. Ashley timidly moved forward and handed Mrs. Kaufman her transfer slip. Mrs. Kaufman slipped her silver-rimmed glasses on and skimmed over the schedule card before she signed it and gave it back to Ashley.

"Is it okay for me to sit at that desk?" Ashley asked. Mrs. Kaufman peered over the top of her glasses following Ashley's finger to the seat behind Cindy. She nodded her silver head and sat down to enter Ashley's name in her grade book and seating chart.

They went over last night's homework and then got back their last quiz. Cindy had gotten only a 71 percent. She'd have to do better than that. Not only would her parents put an end to her swimming if she didn't do well, but she'd never get into a good college. Cindy's love of the beach had convinced her that she wanted to become a marine biologist. And she knew that meant she had to keep her grades up. She forced herself to pay better attention to Mrs. Kaufman. At the end of the class, Cindy wrote down the assignment and gathered her books to go.

"Excuse me." Cindy stopped when she saw Ashley trying to juggle her books and her schedule card and hurrying to catch up to her. "Would you tell me where the biology lab is?"

"Sure. Follow me. I've got Government just around the corner from there." Cindy noticed she was about four or five inches taller than Ashley. In fact, Ashley was about the same size as her little sister, Mollie. Mollie was five-foot-one inches and always wished she were taller.

"I really appreciate this," Ashley told her. "You'd think I'd get used to starting over after six new schools in ten years. But I still hate the feeling of being lost all the time. My dad says this is positively the last move. But then, he says that every time we move."

"Hey, what lunch do you have?" Cindy asked.

Ashley shuffled her notebooks around and looked at her yellow schedule card. "Looks like B."

"Me, too. Why don't we meet you outside the cafeteria and you can sit with us. I'll introduce you to some of the kids, and you won't have to feel like a stranger."

"Thanks a lot." She smiled gratefully and Cindy guessed some orthodontist had made a mint off her parents. No one was born with teeth that perfect.

The rest of the morning was uneventful. Cindy had a five-paragraph essay due on *To Kill a Mockingbird* for English. That meant another weekend of pulling out her hair. She hated writing. If she had her way, Cindy would take only Biology and P.E. She loved being outdoors, and one of the lures of marine biology was that she wouldn't have to spend her life inside. Instead, her work would take her to the beach or out on the water.

The lunch bell rang, and Cindy worked her way through the crowd of kids toward the cafeteria. Someone yelled her name, and she saw her younger sister, Mollie, wave to her. Then Cindy watched Mollie turn her huge flirtatious eyes toward the boy she was walking with. Cindy wasn't sure who he was. She thought he was a junior, but she really didn't know his name for sure. Cindy watched the back of Mollie's long curly blond hair bounce down the hall. She could see why boys were drawn to Mollie. Not only was she cute, she was a born flirt.

"Hi, Cindy. Sorry I took so long," Ashley said from behind her. Cindy turned around.

"Hi. Have any trouble finding it?"

"Actually, I did. I got turned around and ended up in the gym instead. I had to double back against the crowd. I felt like a salmon swimming upstream."

Cindy smiled. "Usually you can smell which one you're closer to. If you smell chlorine, it's the gym and the pool. If it smells like burnt toast, you're near the cafeteria!" She shifted her books in her arm. "Come on. I'll introduce you to everyone."

Cindy saw Duffy's tall frame and his unmistakable flaming red hair as he moved among the tables, balancing a tray. Cindy brought Ashley over to the table. Next to Duffy, who was now over six feet tall, Ashley looked like one of the seven dwarfs. Cindy still couldn't quite get used to Duffy's being so tall. They had been friends forever, and she remembered back to junior high when she was taller than he. He'd caught up with her last year. Now she had stopped at five-foot-six inches, and he was still getting taller.

"This is Ashley Corbett. She just moved here from Oregon. This is her first day here, so don't do anything gross," she warned her table of friends. "This is Duffy, Carey, Anna, Mike, and that's Jason." Cindy threw her books on the floor next to a chair. "Come on. Put your things down, and I'll show you what they're passing off as food today."

Cindy showed Ashley the salad bar and then

the hot lunch line. "It's not so bad, really." she admitted. "You can buy à la carte if you don't want the whole thing. They usually have a couple of choices, too. It's not Taco Rio, but it beats being hungry."

By the time they got back to the table, Cindy's boyfriend, Grant, was there. "Hi." Cindy smiled at him and sat down beside him. He was wearing a new blue sweater that really set off his sparkling blue-green eyes, dark curly hair, and Cindy wondered how she and Grant had ever gotten together. They were both avid surfers, and at first she thought that was what drew him to her. But after several months together, she knew it was more than that.

Grant leaned over and gave her a quick kiss. "How's everything going? Did you get your geometry done?"

"Barely," Cindy answered.

"No thanks to me," Ashley chimed in. Grant looked over at her.

"Oh, I almost forgot. This is Ashley Corbett. Ashley, this is Grant MacPhearson. He just moved here this year, too."

"Oh, really? Where from?" Ashley asked, sitting down across from him at the table.

"Hawaii."

"No kidding? I thought leaving Oregon was bad, but leaving a place like Hawaii must have been terrible."

"Oh, there are some things I like better here."

Grant winked at Cindy and put his arm around her.

"Don't let him fool you. The real reason he likes it here is because the California waves are so much better for surfing," Duffy teased.

"Oh, wow, are you a surfer?" Ashley asked.

"Yeah. I guess we all are. Cindy is one of the best there is." Cindy felt herself blush at the praise. It meant even more coming from Grant, who was one of the best surfers she'd ever seen. Right after he had moved from Santa Barbara, Cindy had beaten him in a surfing contest she'd been pushed into. Of course, she had won because she was lucky enough to catch a great wave. She looked at Grant's blue-green eyes and decided she'd been lucky in more ways than one.

"Hey, Lewis, when you two get done over there, I'd like to talk to you," Duffy said. He bit into his thick ham sandwich and grinned with satisfaction.

"What do you want?" Cindy said.

"I heard Roscoe has some new drill he picked up from Foresthill that's a real killer." Roscoe was their swim coach. He was built like the Pillsbury Dough Boy, but his looks were deceiving. There was nothing soft about him. "Yeah," he continued, "guess he's more than a little worried about that big meet with Newport Beach next Tuesday."

"That's coming up fast," Cindy agreed. "Scary, isn't it?"

"Not as scary as your missing practice again between now and then," Duffy said with a twinkle in his green eyes. Duffy knew her last missed practice hadn't been entirely Cindy's fault. Her locker had jammed, so she was late for Government class. Mr. Cosgrove gave her a detention that no amount of pleading or bargaining could abolish.

"Hey, enough jock talk already," Grant said. "You're putting the rest of us to sleep."

Duffy stuffed his empty sandwich wrapper into his lunch sack. "Okay," he said, "we'll talk Ashley. So you're from Oregon, huh?" he said, turning to her.

"Yeah," she said, a blush creeping into her cheeks when she saw all the attention at the table focused on her.

"Which do you like better?" Jason asked. "Oregon or California?"

"Hey, that's really putting her on the spot!" Cindy laughed. "Besides, she hasn't been here long enough to form an opinion yet. Give her a chance."

"Well, I love it here," Grant said, "but I know how tough it is to move. You make plans, and you expect to be with the same kids till you graduate. Then suddenly everything changes. You go someplace else, and you have to start all over again. It's not easy making new friends and different plans."

"And sometimes you're afraid to make any plans at all," Ashley said softly. "Because you never know when you'll have to leave again."

The bell rang, and everyone began gathering

up trays and trash to deposit on the way out. Cindy felt something for Ashley she couldn't quite figure out. Sympathy? Compassion? Ashley didn't seem like Cindy's other friends. But for some reason, Cindy was drawn to her. Maybe it was her resemblance to Mollie.

"Hey, I've got an idea," Cindy said on the way out of the cafeteria. "Why don't you come over tomorrow after school? It's Thursday, and we usually don't have long practice. You can just wait for me, if you want to, and then we'll go to my house afterward."

"Oh, Cindy, that sounds terrific!" Ashley said brightly.

"If anything happens and you can't make it, we'll do it some other time," Cindy assured her.

"I'm sure it'll be okay. My mother is so busy right now with decorators and workmen and moving she won't even notice I'm gone."

"Then it's all set," Cindy said.

"The next afternoon Grant dropped Cindy and Ashley off at Cindy's house. "Want to come in?" Cindy asked.

"Can't. I promised my dad I'd mow the lawn and take care of the pool. Then he promised me that if I forgot, I'd be grounded this weekend."

"Good incentive." Cindy kissed him before she jumped out of the car.

"I'll call you tonight," he said.

"See ya," Cindy said, shutting the door of his shiny red Trans Am. She waved as he pulled out of the driveway.

"You're so lucky. He's really a doll," Ashley said. "And I don't just mean his looks. He's so nice."

"He sure is," Cindy admitted. "Come on in. I'll show you around." They went up the walk toward the Lewises' house. It was a roomy white stucco house topped by a red-tile roof. Like the other houses in their Santa Barbara neighborhood, it had a slightly Spanish flavor.

"Anybody home?" Cindy's voice echoed through the silent house and bounced off the walls.

"Just me," Mollie said, coming around the corner from the kitchen. She was wearing a red jogging suit she'd filched from their older sister, Nicole. The bright red seemed to put an even brighter glow in her already rosy cheeks. Mollie was eating a container of yogurt.

"What happened to the banana diet?" Cindy asked.

"The ones at the store looked awful, so I bought this." She held up the container for them to see. Mollie was always trying some great new diet and never stuck with any of them.

"This is Ashley Corbett," Cindy said. "My little sister, Mollie. Let's go in the kitchen and get a snack."

Ashley followed Cindy into the kitchen. Mollie trailed along behind them. "Are you new to Vista?" she asked.

"Yes."

"How do you like it?"

"So far, it's great."

"Where'd you move from?"

"Oregon, this time."

"I bet you loved it there," Mollie said.

"I did once I got used to it. But it was hard leaving Vermont."

"Oh, wow, how many places have you lived?"

"Six, counting this one." Ashley sighed. She certainly didn't seem very excited about it, Cindy thought as she rummaged through the refrigerator for something to eat.

"But who would be happy about trying to make six new sets of friends?" Cindy called from behind the fridge door.

"Nothing for me, thanks, unless you have a diet drink or something," Ashley said.

"There's some Diet Sprite in there," Mollie volunteered. "That's all, I think," she confided to Ashley.

"Unless you find something else, like a milk shake," Cindy added.

Mollie took the cold can from Cindy and whisked it over to the counter, where she handed it to Ashley. Cindy stood up balancing a bowl of chicken salad and a jar of pickles while she swung the door closed. Looking over at Ashley, Cindy saw she and Mollie were nearly the same size, no more than five-foot-one. Maybe little people had to be careful about how much they ate.

"Aren't you having dinner tonight?" Ashley asked.

"Oh, she always eats like that. At supper she'll fill her plate like someone who hasn't eaten in days."

"Yeah, but unlike some people I know, I keep active, so I swim it off instead of diet it off."

"Must be nice," Ashley said longingly. She noticed the pot on the table that Mollie had made in ceramics. "That's beautiful. It looks handmade." Ashley carefully picked it up and started to examine it more closely.

"It is. I made it," Mollie declared proudly.

"I'd love to learn how to do this. It looks like so much fun."

"I'm not into it as much as I used to be," Mollie admitted.

"Too bad. You're good," Ashley told her as she put the pot back on the table.

"Come on," Cindy said. "Let's go on up to my room." Ashley got up from the stool and said good-bye to Mollie and followed Cindy upstairs. Cindy's wall was adorned with medals and trophies from various sporting events: surfing, swimming, water polo, softball. Ashley moved over for a closer look.

"Did you win all these?"

"Yup." Cindy tried to act indifferent. She certainly won enough things so she should be used to people making a fuss. But she still got embarrassed by people who thought it was a big deal.

"Duffy and Grant weren't kidding about you being good, were they? Oh, Cindy, do you think you could teach me how to surf?" she asked, her deep blue eyes sparkling.

"Sure. It's not that tough."

"It doesn't look like anything's too tough for

you. The rest of us might not be so lucky. But I still want to learn how. I always like to do things that are typical of the places we live. When we were in Vermont, I learned to ski. In Oregon, I went salmon fishing. Now I'll surf."

"Okay. I'll start your lessons on Saturday."

"Thanks. I may not turn out to be much of an expert in any one thing, but I'll certainly be versatile." Ashley laughed.

They heard a knock at the door, and Mrs. Lewis stuck her head in. Smokey, one of the Lewises' cats, took advantage of the opening to slip in the room. "What's going on?" Mrs. Lewis asked.

"Hi, Mom. This is Ashley Corbett. Ashley, my mom. Ashley just moved here from Oregon."

"Well, we hope you like it here," her mother said with a welcoming smile. "Would you like to stay for supper? I'm trying a new recipe for lasagna, and it feeds an army. I'm giving it a trial run here before taking it to the public."

"I'll call my mom and ask. Thanks for inviting me."

"You're welcome. I'll be down in the kitchen. Let me know if you can stay," her mom said as she shut the door.

Ashley turned to Cindy. "Your mom is so nice. I can't believe she'd just invite me to stay over like that."

"My mom loves to cook," Cindy said. "And just about everything she makes is terrific. That's why Dad talked her into opening a catering business, Movable Feasts."

"That's a great name," Ashley said.

"We think so. It's kind of a family thing. Mom cooks, Nicole helps, and the rest of us are the taste testers."

"Doesn't she ever come up with bad stuff?"

"Not really. I guess there was one time that she had a special request for a Saint Patrick's Day party and she used spinach noodles and dyed the cheese sauce green to match them. It came out the color of an army tent, but it tasted pretty good."

Ashley laughed. "At least your mother cooks. My mother has one specialty: microwave supreme. If it can't be popped into a microwave and ready in five minutes, we don't eat it. Or else we eat out. It doesn't take long before we're on a first-name basis with every waiter in town, because my mother likes to eat out whenever my father is gone. And *that* is most of the time."

"That sounds like my kind of cooking. I'd love a few nights out, but with our family of five, we usually end up at Burger King."

"Well, sure it's fun for a while," she said seriously. "But it gets old real fast." Ashley got up and went into the hall to use the phone. Cindy could hear the muffled talking from the other side of the door.

Ashley came back into the room and sat on Cindy's bed. "She says it's okay for me to stay. In fact, she's probably already flipping through the Yellow Pages for a restaurant that delivers, since

Dad's working late and she can give the microwave the night off."

Cindy laughed. She went to the top of the stairs.
"Hey, Mom, Ashley's staying for dinner."

"Fine," her mother called back. "We'll eat in
half an hour." Cindy came back in the room and
found Ashley thumbing through one of her old
junior-high yearbooks. Cindy gently lifted Smokey
into her arms and began stroking him behind the
ears. He purred softly.

"Is that really you?" Ashley laughed, pointing
to a freckle-faced girl with braids and a toothy
grin.

"That's me." Ashley looked at the attractive girl
next to her with the blond curls and beautiful
skin and thought Cindy had certainly changed in
the past few years.

"That's nothing," Cindy said, sitting beside her.
"Wait till you see Duffy." She pulled the book
over and flipped to the page with Duffy's picture.
A freckled kid with a mouthful of braces and hair
standing up on end grinned at her. Ashley broke
into gales of laughter.

"I don't believe it! He's so much cuter now."

"I'd like to think we all are," Cindy said.

Ashley closed the book gently and put it down.
"It must be nice to stay in one place long enough
to see how your friends change." The same sadness Cindy had seen at lunch the day before
crept into her face.

The sadness disappeared as Mollie bounced

into the room. "C'mon, you two, dinner's almost ready," Mollie said.

They followed her down to the kitchen. Nicole, the oldest of the Lewis sisters, was at home by then and helping her mother with dinner by tossing salad and putting it in salad bowls. The lasagna smelled great, and Cindy realized she was starving. "Oh, yeah, Ash, this is my sister Nicole. Nicole, this is Ashley Corbett."

"Bonjour," Nicole said with a wave of a spoon. It was just like Nicole to say hello in French. She loved everything about France, and she practiced speaking French all the time.

Ashley looked at Nicole's flawless complexion framed by her soft brown hair. "Your sister's beautiful," she whispered. "She ought to be a model."

"She is," Cindy said matter-of-factly. It wasn't that Cindy herself wasn't attractive, in a wholesome way but she lacked the patience and interest her other sisters had in beauty and style. It all seemed like such a bore to her.

"Is there anything I can do to help, Mrs. Lewis?" Ashley asked.

Laura Lewis's eyes lit up and she smiled. Most of Cindy's friends weren't as anxious to lend a hand around the kitchen. "Well, thank you. You can put that cheese on the table if you would." Ashley picked up a bowl of grated Parmesan cheese, and Mrs. Lewis said, "Cindy, honey, grab that butter dish and set it on the table, will you?"

Cindy did as her mom asked, then showed Ashley where to sit at the table. Everyone else joined

them, and they dug into the lasagna. The new
recipe was awesome, and even dieting Mollie had
seconds.

"This dinner is wonderful," Ashley said. "I love
that lasagna."

"Would you like the recipe?"

"Well, um. I hate to put you to so much trouble."

"It's not trouble," Mrs. Lewis assured her.

"Actually, my mother doesn't do much cooking." Ashley's face turned pink, and Cindy sensed
her embarrassment.

"Oh, I see. Well, if you ever change your mind,
I'll be happy to copy it down for you."

"Thank you."

"Mollie tells me you're from Oregon," Mr. Lewis
said.

"Yes."

"Beautiful country," he said. "I always thought if
we ever left Santa Barbara, that's where I'd like to
go."

"Are we thinking of moving?" Mollie asked
quickly.

"Of course not," he said. Mollie's face fell, and
she went back to smashing lasagna noodles beneath her fork.

"You're lucky," Ashley said. "At least you know
when you write up your schedule for next year
that you'll be around to take the classes." Mollie
thought about how upset she'd been when she
found she'd be attending a different high school
from all her junior high friends and decided maybe
Ashley had a point.

Ashley helped clear the table and put the dishes in the dishwasher. "You don't have to do that," Cindy said. "It's Mollie's turn to do dishes."

"I don't mind, really."

"Neither do I." Mollie laughed. She smirked at Cindy while Ashley continued to load the dishwasher. Cindy suspected Ashley had made a friend for life.

Later that evening while they were waiting on the porch for Ashley's father, Ashley turned to Cindy and said, "You have the neatest family."

"I do?"

"Well, you're all so beautiful and talented. I mean, it's the kind of family they make television shows about. Everything's perfect."

"You wouldn't think so if you were around here in the morning when all three of us are trying to use the bathroom or some Friday night when we're all fighting over the phone. You're the lucky one. An only child with a whole house to yourself."

"I don't know about that. I think you're pretty lucky, too." Mr. Corbett pulled his BMW into the driveway and honked. "Come on, I want you to meet my dad," Ashley said, pulling Cindy toward the car. "Dad, this is Cindy Lewis. She's about the greatest surfer in Santa Barbara, and she's going to teach me how to surf next week. She's ..."

"That's great, honey. Hop in. I've got a business

review in the morning, and I have to get up early. Nice to meet you, Sandy."

Cindy watched the sparkle in Ashley's eyes fade, and she thought, Maybe I *am* the lucky one, after all.

Chapter 2

*O*n Saturday morning, Cindy bounced out of bed at 6:45, pulled on a pair of sweats, and ran a brush through her short blond hair. She slipped quietly down the stairs into the garage, where she tapped Winston on the head and whispered, "Come on, boy."

Winston was the Lewises' huge black Newfoundland dog. Between his size and his thick fluffy hair, he looked as much like a bear as he did like a dog. He padded happily out onto the driveway behind Cindy. She stopped and slipped her wrist weights in place. Jogging was great for the lungs and legs, but the weights were what gave her the strong arms she needed for surfing.

Cindy began with a gentle trot down the drive and built up speed until she'd reached the beach. There she turned and headed down the shore.

Every once in a while Winston would run ahead of her, and she'd have to change course to keep from tripping over him. At least running with Winston was never boring.

Occasionally Winston would stop altogether to bite at the incoming waves. One time he ran up next to her with seaweed stuck on his whiskers and looked like Fu Manchu. Cindy started to laugh and eventually had to stop and double over at the sight of him. Poor Winston stood and looked at her as if to ask, "What's so funny?" The harder he stared at her, the longer Cindy laughed. Finally she reached out and pulled the wet slippery stuff from his bristly face.

Cindy stood up straight and took several deep breaths of ocean air. She looked out across the water and checked the wave action. It was a perfect day for Ashley's first surfing lesson. The waves were coming in high enough to surf but not high enough to hurt a beginner.

Cindy watched sea gulls dive-bomb the water for food and looked along the shore for any little treasures that might have washed aground during the night. She had been lucky enough to find some really beautiful shells and even a glass fishing ball once in a while. Her early morning jogs put her on the beach before the crowds picked it over.

Cindy sat on her favorite rock. Winston came over and rested his wet sandy head on her leg. "I could never live away from the ocean," she told him. "We're lucky, boy. Some people live their whole lives in places with no beach at all." She checked out the waves one more time, then got to her feet. "Let's go home."

As Cindy started back, she judged it might be close to eight o'clock. She hoped her mother would be up fixing breakfast. On some Saturday and Sunday mornings, her mother got up early and cooked up some pretty fantastic stuff. When the whole family had time for breakfast, she liked to experiment with things like pecan waffles and Mexican omelets. Just thinking about it made Cindy hungry.

She went into the garage and gave Winston fresh food and water. She didn't hear any noises from the kitchen. Slipping off her sandy running shoes, she opened the door. Her heart sank. No great smell greeted her—only an empty kitchen. She'd have to make herself a plain breakfast of bacon and eggs or wait until her mom got up. Her stomach rumbled loudly, and she went into the fridge to get some bacon. One good thing about being an athlete—it let her eat as much as she wanted. If her mother made something later, she'd have some of that, too.

Cindy had just put the last of her breakfast dishes in the dishwasher when the phone began to ring. She quickly wiped her wet hands and picked up the receiver. "Hi, there," Grant said. "Still planning to go to the beach today?"

"Sure."

"I just talked to Duffy, and he thought we ought to get over there by nine-thirty in order to get a good spot. Now that it's warming up, everyone seems to be hitting the beach."

"You're right," Cindy agreed. "Ashley should be calling any minute. Why don't you and Duffy save a good spot? We'll meet you at the beach."

But it was close to ten before Ashley finally called. Cindy kicked herself for not getting Ashley's phone number at school Friday.

"Hi, did I wake you up?" Ashley said.

"I've been up since six-forty-five."

"Are you kidding me? I don't even think my clock runs that early on Saturday mornings, but I've never gotten up to check it for sure." She laughed. "What time do you want to head over to the beach?"

"Anytime. Everyone else is already there."

"I can be ready in about an hour or so." That meant they wouldn't get to the beach until after eleven.

"Tell you what," Cindy said, "why don't you go ahead and get ready, and I'll meet you there?"

"Well, okay," she said hesitantly. "I hope I can find you."

"There'll be a whole bunch of us: Grant, Anna, Carey. Just look for Duffy's red hair if you get lost. It's kind of like a beacon on the shore and you'll be able to track us down."

"Okay. I'll hurry and get ready and meet you there in an hour."

Cindy paddled out into the water and got to her knees to begin the ride back. When the wave she'd been waiting for came up behind her, she stood up and rode it into shore. She glided off into the water and saw Ashley standing on the beach applauding her.

"That's nothing. You ought to see her take a big one," Grant said, coming up behind them.

"Nobody's going to take any big ones today from the looks of things," Cindy said. "But it's a good day for a surfing lesson." She turned to face Ashley. "All ready?"

Ashley nodded hesitantly. Cindy took her out about waist-deep and began by showing her how to get on a surfboard. "First you lean your stomach on the board," she explained. "Then you swing your leg up."

Ashley, being eager to learn, enthusiastically swung her leg up and went right off the side of the board. "Not that much swing," Cindy said, laughing, when Ashley bobbed back up to the surface. "Now try again."

After a couple more unsuccessful tries, Ashley managed to get her midsection and her leg on the elusive board. "Now pull the other leg up," Cindy said.

Anxious not to fall off again, Ashley gripped the board tightly and pulled her leg up. The board tipped and began to roll over. Ashley let out a scream as she went under. Cindy pulled the board back around, and Ashley sputtered to the top, still holding tightly to the board.

"Hey, did you see her turn turtle?" Grant asked Cindy as he waded out toward them.

"Do what?" Ashley coughed.

"Turn turtle," Grant said. "When you're paddling out and a big wave is headed right at you, sometimes the easiest thing to do is go under it. You just grab your board, turn under, and let the wave wash over you."

"But you take a good breath first," Cindy advised Ashley, who was still coughing from her sudden dunking.

Grant said "Here, let me see if I can help you with this getting-on thing." He explained that Ashley needed to get on in three steps and to be careful to stay balanced.

"Grant, you make it sound so easy," Ashley said as she began to wobble back onto the swaying board with uncertainty.

"It is," he assured her. When she was successful lying on the board and it wasn't threatening to tip over, he said, "See what I mean?"

They spend another thirty minutes teaching Ashley how to paddle out across the waves and how to cup her hands to pull her more smoothly through the water.

The real trouble began when Grant tried to teach her how to get up now that she was finally on the board and heading in the right direction. "You have to ease up slowly," he told her. Then he looked at her white knuckles gripping either side of the board. "I have a better idea. Why don't you just try riding your first wave on your stomach?"

Ashley's huge blue eyes showed real fear as

she turned the board and prepared to ride the next wave. They weren't out far, but Ashley looked skeptical of her ability to get back to shore.

"I'll ride with you," Grant said. "Just hold on to the board if you feel yourself slipping. It'll keep you up."

Cindy watched Grant expertly get onto his own board before she began swimming to shore. She turned over on her back and leisurely floated. When she heard Ashley scream, Cindy began to tread water so that she could watch Ashley's first ride.

With a look of concentration on her face and her eyes riveted to the shore, Ashley caught her first wave. It gently lifted her into the air, and she sailed to the bottom of it. Her face broke into a smile. The water rose again, and she began to laugh. She sailed past Cindy and continued in.

Ashley got to the shallow water, where she stood up and grabbed Grant and jumped up and down. Cindy body-surfed in, and Ashley ran over and grabbed her before Cindy ever had a chance to stand up. They both ended up underwater.

"Let's do it again," Ashley begged as she broke the surface, coughing. "That was awesome!"

"Go ahead," Cindy laughed. "Take my board and go on back out with Grant. I'll watch from the shore this time."

"But what about you? Don't you want to surf?"

"I'll catch the next one."

They turned toward the water. Duffy came up beside Cindy and dropped onto the sand next to her. "Looks like you got some competition there, kid."

"I think it'll be a while before she's out-surfing me." Cindy laughed.

"That wasn't the kind of competition I was talking about." He got up and took his own board and went into the water. Cindy wondered if he could possibly mean Ash and Grant. No. That would never happen. Grant was just a better teacher than she was. After all, she'd nearly drowned Ashley, and Grant had gotten her up on the board on the first try.

Cindy vowed not to even think about it and lay back on the sand to watch the clouds float by. She heard Ashley calling her name and sat up. Crouching on her knees, Ashley was making an unsteady ride toward shore. She was smiling as she skimmed over the water. Until she hit a rough spot and rolled over, that was. She came up sputtering, and the board popped away from her and started back without her. Grant pulled in beside her and helped her onto his board and rode them both back to shore. Cindy went to the water's edge and got her board as it washed onto the beach.

"Oh, Grant, it's positively the most thrilling thing I've ever done!" Ashley said as she jumped from his board. "I mean, I thought skiing was kind of scary, but it's nothing like this. You really fly down a ski slope, but at least the mountain doesn't move! With this," Ashley said, turning toward the ocean, "you never know what to expect. It's so unpredictable." She seemed to remember Cindy was standing there and turned around. "I can see why you two love it so much."

"Now you go, Cindy," Ashley said, giving her a gentle push toward the water. "Show me a real pro in action, okay? Besides, I have to catch my breath from the last ride."

"Okay." Cindy took the board and trotted into the water. She paddled out about one hundred yards and then waited for the right wave. She watched the swells and finally saw the one she wanted. The waves weren't high enough today for a fantastic ride, but it would be a fun one. She positioned herself on the board and got to her knees, then she stood up and began moving her weight up and down the board, balancing and turning herself with the balls and heels of her feet. She worked her way to the back of the board and stepped on the tail to lift the nose out of the water as she got to shore. It was really pretty routine, but Ashley seemed impressed.

She started out to meet Cindy at the shoreline. Suddenly she gave a little cry and jumped back, pulling her leg out of the water. She had seaweed on her feet. The way she gingerly removed it reminded Cindy of something Mollie would do. Then the resemblance disappeared as she came closer to Cindy and she was smiling again.

"You make that look so easy," Ashley said.

"You can, too, with a little practice," Cindy told her. "By the end of the summer, you'll be standing up on this thing telling it what to do," she added, tapping her surfboard.

"You think so, huh?"

"Yeah. Why not?" Cindy went and planted her board in the sand. With a whole summer of lessons from Grant and Cindy, anybody could be a good surfer. But first they'd have to teach Ashley not to be afraid of seaweed!

Chapter 3

*W*hile Cindy had been giving a surfing lesson that Saturday morning, Mrs. Lewis was driving Mollie and her friends to the shopping mall. "Now you're sure that Sarah's mother will be able to pick you up?" she asked again as Mollie got out of the car. She wore the same worried look that Nicole had when their parents had gone to China earlier that year and Mollie had tried to give herself a radical new image. Ever since then, Mollie couldn't help noticing how much alike Nicole and her mother were.

"Yes, Mom," she said, "Sarah's mother said she'd be home by three and she'd be waiting for our call."

"Okay, I just want to be sure, because you know your father and I will be leaving the house about two-thirty. We won't get back until late tonight, and I wouldn't want you girls stranded here."

"Come *on*, Mollie," Sarah urged as a cute boy walked by. Sarah stepped aside and tossed her long blond hair in his direction. Sarah shifted her weight restlessly as she waited at the mall door for Mollie.

"I'm coming," she called to Sarah and Linda. "I gotta go, Mom. I'll see you tonight." Mollie ran up to join the girls. They went into the mall chattering excitedly about what they would do with an entire day to themselves.

"I want to try on everything in Nordstrom's junior department," Sarah said. "My mother is always wrinkling her nose at everything I pick out and asking me if I really *like* it."

"I know what you mean," Linda piped up. "Last week my mom brought home the ugliest pair of pants you've ever seen and actually expected me to wear them. Then she got all bent out of shape when I told her what I thought of them. She said that I was getting too hard to please lately these days." She shook her head in desperation.

"Hold it," Sarah said, putting her hand out to stop her friends. "Do you see what I see?"

Both girls looked in the direction Sarah was looking and saw the chocolate specialty shop, Sweet Dreams. "Well?" Sarah asked with a mischievous grin.

"But it's only ten-thirty," Linda protested. "We haven't even had lunch yet."

"Who's acting like a mother now?" Sarah said.

"You're right," Linda agreed. "Who's going to know if we stuff ourselves on candy? We can even skip lunch!" Her eyes lit up, and she followed the chocolate smell into the store.

Mollie thought briefly about the water diet she'd read about and that she had been planning to start. Oh, well, that could wait until Monday. This might provide a challenge for her. After all, if she did gain an extra pound or two this weekend, she'd be more desperate to take it off next week. Maybe she'd stick to the new diet longer.

"Oh, wow!" Linda said, her eyes growing wide. "Look at those nut clusters." She moved to the glass display case, never once glancing away from the inviting chocolates.

"Personally, I like these caramels." Sarah said, pointing to the case. "What about you, Mollie?"

Everything looked and smelled delicious. Mollie wanted one of each. "I think they all look great."

"They are," the clerk said.

"Then in that case, I can't go wrong. I'll take one of these and one of those and that and one of the pink in the back...." Mollie continued to point to candies until she saw the amount due on the scale. She made a quick tally of her funds. "Guess you'd better put that last one back," she told the clerk.

They roamed around the mall and checked out the store windows while they ate. They ended up on a bench in the center of the mall. "Oh, my gosh, look at that," Linda said in a voice that must have carried a mile.

Sarah and Mollie spun around to see. "Don't look now!" She squealed. Both girls snapped their heads forward.

"What is it we're supposed to look at without moving our eyes?" Mollie asked.

"Him?"

"Who?"

"That guy over there in the goofy-looking shirt. I didn't think anyone dressed like that these days." She was laughing and trying not to show it. The boy looked over at them, and Mollie felt a pang of sympathy for him.

A gray-haired man wearing a three-piece suit came by, and Mollie said, "That's the kind of man I'm going to marry."

"Old?" Linda asked with a giggle.

"No," Mollie retorted. "Distinguished. Can't you just tell he's successful?"

"I think all that chocolate has gone to your head," Sarah said. "Let's see if we can walk it off."

They dropped their candy sacks in the garbage and wiped the chocolate from their hands before heading toward Nordstrom's. The junior department was at the back of the store, so they tried on hats and scarves along the way. When they finally got to the back of the store, Mollie raced instantly to a new display of sportswear.

"May I help you?" the saleslady asked as she noticed Mollie burdened with several items.

"I'd like to try these on." She thrust the bundle of clothes and hangers toward the salesclerk.

"You can only take three items in the dressing room at a time. If you'd like, I'll hang these out here and you can change them as you need to." Mollie picked the thing out she wanted to try on first.

Mollie tried on a cream-and-turquoise sweat suit with a matching tank top. She liked it all right, but it didn't really do anything magical for her. She wanted something more colorful. Besides, sweat suits were so big on her petite frame that she tended to get lost in them.

She tried on another outfit that she liked much better. She was evaluating herself in the mirror when Sarah opened the door of her dressing room and stepped out. "Mollie, you look terrific in that!"

"You really think so?" she asked, turning from side to side to get a better look at herself in the three-way mirror. The blue paisley did set off her eyes, and the pants accentuated her slim waist. She had to admit it was cute. But she knew it had a cute price tag, too. She could just see herself trying to talk her mom into this outfit.

After a while all three girls got bored trying on clothes and told the saleslady they would be back with their mothers. When Mollie asked her to hold the outfit she liked, the lady smiled. "Good luck talking your parents into it," she said pleasantly. Giggling wildly, the trio left the department.

Next they went into Merle Norman Cosmetics and began looking over the makeup. The saleslady was busy giving a facial to a customer who said she had come in looking fifty but wanted to leaving looking thirty.

The girls took advantage of the situation to do a little experimenting on their own. "Here," Mollie said, turning Sarah to face her, "let me show you this thing I saw in *Seventeen* to make your eyes look bigger."

"What's wrong with my eyes?" Sarah asked defensively as she pulled the mirror around for a closer look.

"Not a thing!" Linda said.

"Yeah, this just accents your eyes. It makes anybody look terrific," Mollie said.

"Have you tried it?" Sarah wanted to know. "Your eyes don't look any bigger to me."

"I don't have the right colors at home," Mollie said.

"Well, okay. But don't you dare make me look dumb, Mollie Lewis."

"I won't," she insisted. Mollie set to work, and Sarah's eyes did seem to get larger. Linda got enthusiastic and wanted Mollie to do her next.

"Looks like you're after my job," the salesgirl said.

"Oh, no," Mollie said, feeling herself blush. "You looked busy, so we thought we'd experiment."

"That's okay. But I'm not busy now. Do you girls want to see something special?"

"Oh, no," Sarah said. "We have to meet someone now at the fountain. Thanks, anyway."

"Yeah, thanks," Mollie echoed.

"Come again," the girl said, but you could tell it was the kind of thing she said to everyone and she didn't care if they came again or not.

"Oh, look," Linda exclaimed. She was standing in front of the pet store. "Let's go inside and hold the puppies." The store window had several puppies in it. They watched two cocker spaniels play with each other for a minute before they went into the store.

The girls stopped just inside the door, and Mollie's attention was drawn to the register. She noticed a tall, attractive boy with light brown hair and a gorgeous smile. The cute little puppies bouncing energetically in their cages for her attention didn't have a chance.

"Oh, boy! Will you look at that?" Linda said.

"I'm looking," Mollie whispered. "I'm looking."

"Have you ever seen anything so adorable?"

"Not in a long time," Mollie said, remembering the ski team she'd met during her family's ski trip last Christmas.

"Wouldn't you love it if he was yours?" Linda sighed.

"You've got to be kidding. My mother would die," Sarah said.

"My sisters would die," Mollie said.

"What do you think he is?" Sarah said skeptically as she peered toward the register.

Mollie looked at her in confusion. "I'd say he's a junior. Maybe even a senior."

"What?" Linda said, turning to stare at Mollie.

"Who's a senior? What are you talking about?" Sarah asked.

"*He* is," Mollie said, nodding toward the register. "What are you talking about?"

"That puppy over there in the pen." Linda pointed to a small pen next to the checkout counter. There was a strange-looking little gray dog standing in the corner. He looked terrified by the people who were gathered around staring at him.

"What are *you* talking about?" Linda said.

"The guy behind the counter," Mollie said in exasperation.

"*What* guy?" Linda said. Now it was her turn to be confused. Mollie looked toward the counter, but he wasn't there anymore.

Suddenly he popped up from behind the cash register where he had been kneeling. "That guy!" Mollie said smugly.

"He is cute," Sarah agreed. The three of them moved into the store and went to the pen that was drawing so much attention. Mollie reached down and gently patted the bony frame of the little dog. He turned his woeful eyes on them and cocked his floppy ears at either side of his long narrow face.

"I think he's ugly," Sarah said hesitantly.

"Yeah, but look at that face. He's so homely he's cute." Mollie bent over to get a closer look. "He kind of grows on you ... like E.T."

"I guess," Sarah said without sounding too convinced.

"You can pick him up if you'd like." Mollie got to her feet and turned to discover she was standing almost face-to-face with the gorgeous guy from behind the counter. He was even better-looking up close. He had the kind of all-American face that belonged on a cereal box. His eyes were soft brown with flecks of gold in them, just like his hair.

"What is that?" asked Sarah, pointing to the dog and trying hard to keep the disgust out of her voice.

"An Italian greyhound."

"Poor little thing," Mollie said. "It looks like it's starving."

"They're supposed to be that way. They generally weigh only about six to eight pounds and stand twelve inches high."

"I've never seen one before."

"Most people haven't," he told her. "They're a very old, rare breed. Skeletons of these dogs were found in the Egyptian pharaohs tombs. In fact, did you know the saying Beware of Dog was actually because of these little guys?" He picked up the thin little creature, who immediately snuggled in next to him.

"They were lapdogs of royalty. To make sure no one stepped on their pets, they put up a sign BEWARE OF DOG."

"That's fascinating," Mollie said, batting her big blue eyes at him. "How do you know so much about dogs?" Mollie watched as his hand gently rubbed the velvety ears on the miniature animal.

"Oh, I hope to be a vet one day. I learn all I can about every breed we sell."

"That's wonderful," Mollie said. "I love dogs, too. We have a Newfoundland named Winston."

"They're great dogs. Does he like the water?"

"Oh, yeah, in fact I take him to the beach all the time." Actually it was Cindy who usually took Winston for his run.

Signaling Mollie that they were ready to move on, Sarah gently nudged her. Mollie, who was captivated by the boy's handsome face, lost her balance and almost fell onto him. She put her hand out to catch herself and put it right on his nametag. Greg Masters. He caught her by the arm with one strong hand and carfully balanced the frail puppy in the other.

"Are you all right?" he asked.

"I'm sorry," Mollie said, feeling herself blush. "I felt dizzy for a moment."

"Here," he said, setting the dog back in the pen and taking a firmer grip on her arm. "Do you need to sit down?"

"No. I'm fine now." She glanced over at Sarah and Linda, who had moved toward the front of the store. Both of them looked like they might burst out laughing at any minute. If they did, Mollie vowed she would never speak to either of them again.

"Well, if you're sure," he said, reluctantly letting go of her arm. "You know, I love Newfoundlands. I have a golden myself."

"A golden?" Mollie said.

"A golden retriever."

"Oh, yes, yes, of course. A *golden*."

"We run along the beach, too. Usually down around Milton's Point. Do you know that area?"

"Sure! That's not far from where I live."

"Really? Maybe we could run together some morning. You do run in the mornings, don't you?"

"Mostly, yeah."

"Well, I think there's nothing quite like the sounds of the early morning surf to start your day off right."

"Right," Mollie said, knowing she was getting herself in deeper every minute. She had to do it, though, or risk losing the attention of the best-looking guy she'd seen in a long time.

'Greg," a lady said from behind the display counter, "could you help me with these display items?"

"Yeah, of course." He turned back to Mollie. "Well, it's been great talking to you, uh . . ."

"Mollie Lewis."

"I'm Greg Masters. I'll look for you on the beach." He disappeared into the back room, and Mollie wondered if she'd ever seen him again.

Chapter 4

"*Hey, Cin, wait up,*" *Duffy called. Cindy turned* around and saw him trying to make his way through the milling students, who, unlike Cindy, were in no hurry to get to sixth period.

Cindy continued to walk backward, occasionally bumping into kids as she went. The ones who knew her said hi and the ones who didn't told her to watch where she was going.

"Wait up," he called again.

"Can't. We're already late. Put a move on, or we're both busted." Cindy had intended to get to the gym before the fifth-period bell rang. Coach Roscoe had everyone released ten minutes before the bell so they'd have time to get to the gym and prepare for the upcoming meet with Newport Beach before the halls filled with kids. It was amazing how fast the weekend shot by and Tuesday was upon them.

She'd gotten out of class on time, but as she was coming around the corner by the counselor's office, she saw Ashley. "You coming to the meet this afternoon?" Cindy asked.

"I want to, but my parents are going out tonight, and I wouldn't have a way home." She sighed.

"No problem. Grant and I can give you a ride."

Ashley's face lifted into a smile. "Cindy, I swear you're the greatest!" Ashley gave her a quick hug, which made Cindy feel a little awkward toward Cindy. Nicole and Mollie were the huggers. Cindy was more the sock-on-the-arm type. The bell rang and Ashley sped off toward her classroom to get her books. Cindy saw the halls filling with students and knew she'd be late to the gym.

Duffy finally managed to break free and catch up to Cindy. "How come you're running late?" she asked him.

"Test in Geometry. It was major."

"I know. Mine's tomorrow. How'd you do?"

"I think I blew it."

"Oh, well, cheer up," she said. "You won't be ineligible until next week, and the match with Newport Beach will be over by then."

"That's what I like about you, kid." He draped his arm around her shoulders. "You're such an optimist."

"That's me," she said, breaking off and pushing

through the door to the girl's locker room. "Little Cindy Sunshine."

"Give me a break," he yelled as the heavy metal door clanged shut behind her.

A short while later, Cindy stepped into the pool area and felt her heart speed up at the sound of the swimmers hitting the water and the smell of the chlorine. She always felt nervous and excited just before a meet. She placed her goggles on her face and glanced up at the clock. She had thirty minutes to warm up.

"Lewis, you're late!" Coach Roscoe barked. "You're just lucky I don't want to wear you out or you'd be doing extra laps."

"Thanks, Coach."

"Don't thank me. You can work it off after practice tomorrow. Now warm up."

An hour and a half later, Cindy was wishing she had swum laps. At least then she'd have an excuse for her performance. She'd come in second in freestyle and third in the hundred-meter back stroke. Her timing was off. She kept glancing at the bleachers where Grant and Ashley sat watching her, and that made it even worse. The score was much too close to keep lousing up.

Cindy had one event left. Breaststroke. All her years of surfing had given her good upper-body strength, and this was her strongest event. She got off the bench, and as she passed the coach, he said, "Loosen up, kid. Let me see that winning style, okay?"

"Yeah." Cindy nodded, checking out the Newport Beach swimmers lining up along the side.

"Look, forget about the other events. They're history. Just concentrate on what you need to do right now, okay?"

She nodded again. She knew she could do it. She had to just clear everything out of her head and swim.

Cindy stood at the edge of the water and shook out her arms and legs to relax her tense muscles. "Concentrate, Lewis," she whispered to herself. She shut her eyes and blocked out the shouts and the whistles of the cheering crowd. She bent forward, tensed and ready to spring. The gun sounded, and she hit the water.

She felt the power surge through her as she cut through the water. The other swimmers weren't important anymore. She was working only against the clock. Her body fell into the right rhythm, and she pushed herself even harder.

Cindy surfaced at the end of the event and heard a roar from the crowd that confirmed what she already knew. She'd won first place. She pulled herself from the water and felt good for the first time all afternoon.

As the meet drew to a close, they were ahead of Newport Beach with just one event left. Coach Roscoe paced the side of the pool, his eyes dancing back and forth between the scoreboard and the pool. The school that won this relay would win the meet.

The swimmers shot past Cindy. She was on her

feet, straining to see the finish line. The crowd roared, and she knew Vista had won. The broad grin on Roscoe's face confirmed it.

Cindy came out of the locker room to find Grant and Ashley waiting. Grant came forward and put his arm around her. His lips gently brushed hers. "Way to go, babe."

"You must have missed the first half of the meet," she said, tossing her gym bag over her shoulder.

"Don't be so hard on yourself. Your timing was off, but you got it back when it really counted." He slipped his arm around her, and they walked out of the gym area together.

"Yeah, I guess you're right," she said, smiling up at him. There was no use hitting herself over the head for something that was over and done with.

Duffy and Carey were coming out from the other side of the gym. "Hey," Duffy called, "you guys want to grab a pizza?"

"Sounds good," Grant said. Then he looked at Cindy. "That okay with you?"

"Sure. Hey, Ash, you want to grab a pizza with us?"

"Yeah. My folks are out, and I'd probably end up with a frozen dinner anyway." She looked at the others and said, "You sure you don't mind me tagging along?"

"Of course not," Grant said. And the five of them went out into the school parking lot to pile into Grant's car.

They came into Pizza Pete's, and Cindy heard

Jason yell, "It's the girl wonder!" She shook her head and went on up with Grant to order.

They sat down with everyone while they waited for their number to be called. "Well, I'm sure glad that's over," Duffy said. "The tension of this meet always wears me out."

"Must drain Cindy, too," Jason said. "She sure sandbagged long enough."

"Sandbagged?" Cindy said in disbelief.

"Sure. You could've won any one of those events, and you held back to make it more exciting for the rest of us. What a great kid." He patted her on the arm.

"That wasn't it," Cindy said, pulling her arm back.

"Yeah, well, whatever you were doing in the first half of the meet, don't do it again real soon, okay?" Duffy said, getting in on the teasing.

"Yeah, take a little pressure off the rest of us," Jason said.

"Cut it out, you guys," Ashley interrupted. "Cindy isn't superwoman. Why don't you lay off? So she had a bad afternoon. I mean, she *did* come in first in the breaststroke."

Everyone stared at Ashley in stunned silence for a minute. Cindy had known they were all teasing. If it didn't bother her, it shouldn't have mattered, to Ashley.

"We didn't mean anything by it," Duffy said with a shrug.

"I know," Cindy said. "Forget it, Ash. We always kid with each other like this. Why, if Duffy had been the one messing up out there today, we'd all be ribbing him right now."

"I'm sorry." The redness crept into Ashley's face. "I guess I got carried away." She pushed her chair back from the table and got up. "Excuse me," she said, rushing toward the bathroom.

Cindy watched her go, then got up to follow her. Anna looked at Cindy. "Want me to go with you?"

"No. I'm sure it'll be okay. That's our pizza they're calling. Stay here and eat. We'll be right back."

Ashley was leaning against the sink, her lower lip trembling. "Relax! It's no big deal," Cindy said.

"I just feel so stupid. I don't know why I always say the wrong thing. It's just that you're so great, and I hate to see them rub it in because you had a bad day."

"Look, the only one who's bothered by it right now is you. So shake it off! Come on back out and eat before those guys finish it all! I don't know about you, but I'm starving."

"So what else is new?" Ashley said, and they both laughed.

They dropped Ashley off about eight-thirty. Grant turned to Cindy and kissed her briefly. "Let's go to the beach for a little while," he suggested.

Cindy did have that geometry test the next day, and she knew she should be studying for it, but she really wanted to be alone with Grant. "Sure, why not?"

They got out of the car and began to walk hand in hand along the sand. Cindy slipped her shoes off and played tag with the incoming waves. Grant joined her, and soon they were kicking water on each other and running up and down the beach. Cindy slipped on a patch of seaweed and went down into the sand. Grant dropped beside her.

He rested his strong elbow near her face and looked down into her eyes. Then he kissed her gently. Cindy leaned back against the sand and stared up at the night. He rolled over on his back and lay next to her.

"It's so peaceful out here, isn't it?" she asked.

"Um-hmmmm." The waves were gently lapping at the bottoms of their feet. Cindy felt the cool water and the evening breezes.

"It's great to get away like this," Grant said, rolling over toward Cindy and leaning on one elbow. Cindy looked into his handsome face. The glow of the moonlight caught his crystal-blue eyes. "I mean Ashley's okay, and everything, but it feels like this is the first time we've been alone together in a long time. I like being alone with you again." He twirled one of her loose curls in his fingers and studied her face in the blue-white light of the moon.

"I know what you mean," she said, putting her arms around him and pulling him down to her for a kiss. She knew she should be home studying, but right then she couldn't think of any place she'd rather be than lying on the moonlit beach in Grant's arms.

Chapter 5

*A*fter their usual short Thursday practice, Cindy sat on the couch with a big bowl of popcorn on her lap. Smokey and Cinders sat on either side of her, purring happily. The cable sports network was showing an old ski jump competition. A skier flew down the mountain and shot off the jump. He soared skillfully above the snow, then landed safely at the bottom jump. This made even surfing look tame! Cindy decided to look into ski jumping the next time she hit the slopes.

The next skier stood at the gate. Cindy heard the phone ringing. "Hey, Mollie, get that, will you?" she called. It was probably for her anyway.

"It's for you," Mollie said from the doorway. "I don't know why you wouldn't get it yourself. I was trying a new makeup technique."

"I was busy," Cindy said. She went into the kitchen and lifted the receiver. "Hello."

"Cindy, it's Ashley. I couldn't wait to call you. Guess what? My dad's going on a business trip to San Francisco this week, and he and my mother are meeting in San Simeon next weekend."

"That's nice," Cindy said, wondering why she was missing the next ski jump for a report on Ashley's parents' social life.

"Oh, that's not why I called," she went on to say. "They said I could come and I could invite a friend, and of course I thought of you. How about it?"

Cindy perked up. San Simeon. It was a little beach resort about two hours from Santa Barbara. "San Simeon? This weekend, huh?"

"Yes, Dad's booked us our own room and everything. We're staying at this great hotel right on the beach, and then Saturday we're going to tour Hearst Castle. It'll be so much fun. Please say you'll come."

Cindy didn't have a swim meet this weekend or any other special plans. In fact, she couldn't think to miss what sounded like a fun weekend.

"It sounds great to me," Cindy said, "but I have to ask my folks first. I'll call you back later after they get home."

"Okay. But call me right away as soon as you know anything. My parents want to get everything set."

"I will," Cindy promised. She went back into the den. Mollie was sitting on the floor eating

Cindy's popcorn. "Who was that?" she asked between handfuls.

"Ashley. And give me back my popcorn. Go
make your own."

"You know I always burn it"

"What's to burn? You pour it in the popper and
pull the plug when it quits popping." She took the
bowl from Mollie.

"Okay. Be selfish. But I'm not sharing with you,"
Mollie said as she flounced into the kitchen.

"Why not?" Cindy called after her. "You ate
half of mine." She settled in to watch the rest of
the ski jumping and found they had switched
over to women's figure skating. Cindy reached for
the remote control and began flipping through
the channels. She wanted something a bit more
exciting to watch.

It didn't seem like very long before Cindy heard
a desperate cry from the kitchen. "Cindy! Help!
Come quick!"

She jumped to her feet and dashed around the
corner, skidding to a stop on the kitchen floor in
her stocking feet. Popcorn was all over the floor
and popping out at crazy angles around the
kitchen. Mollie was holding the clear plastic lid in
her hand.

"Make it stop!" she cried to Cindy.

Cindy dashed over and grabbed the lid from
Mollie and set it back on the popper. She reached
across the counter and pulled the plug.

"How come you took the lid off, dummy?" Cindy
snapped.

Mollie, her lower lip quivering, answered, "Well, it started running out of the sides. I must have put too much popcorn in. I thought if I took some of it out, the rest of it could pop better."

"How much popcorn did you use?" Cindy asked, looking at the mess around the kitchen.

"About a cup, I guess."

"You guess? Didn't you measure it? Mollie, didn't you even read the directions? They're right here on the jar." Cindy grabbed the jar and pointed to the label.

"But you said to just pour it in and unplug it when it stops popping."

"But I thought you'd know enough to read the directions first. Can't you do anything right?" Cindy asked with annoyance. She brushed some of the popcorn from the counter into a bowl. "Go get a broom, and I'll help you get this cleaned up."

"Just remember you owe me one," Cindy said.

By the time they'd swept up the floor and cleaned off the counter, Mollie had calmed down.

Mrs. Lewis opened the back door just as Cindy was dumping the last of the popcorn into the garbage. "Have an accident?" she asked.

"More like a cooking lesson," Cindy answered.

Mollie looked at her sister, smiled, and mouthed, "Thanks!" with a look of relief.

"Well, if you're done in here, I've got a carful of groceries I could use some help with," Mrs. Lewis said, setting down a bag.

"Hey, Mom," Cindy said as she brought in the last bag of groceries and set them on the counter,

"Ashley called and invited me to go to San Simeon for the weekend with her parents. They'll pay for everything, so it won't be expensive. Do you think it will be okay?"

"We'll have to check with your dad. I'm not sure about you going out of town with people we haven't met yet," Cindy folded up one empty bag and began unloading another. She was trying to think of some way to convince her mother to let her go, but she thought it was better not to push it any further. She might have an easier time convincing her dad anyhow.

It was another hour before her dad got home. She was in her room when she heard his voice down in the kitchen. She took the steps two at a time and ran into the kitchen as her mother was going out. "Guess what?" she said, hopping easily onto the counter top and dangling her legs.

"What?" he said, opening the fridge and getting out the orange juice. He poured a glass for himself.

"Ashley asked me to go to San Simeon for the weekend, and Mom said to ask you."

"I see." He took a long drink from the glass before filling it again. "Who else is going?"

"Her parents are taking us." She got down off the counter. "What do you say, Dad?"

"What did your mother say?"

"She said to ask you."

"*And* she said she's not sure about you taking a trip with a family she doesn't know," her mother said sternly, coming into the kitchen behind her.

"Aw, Mom," Cindy said, turning to her mother. "C'mon, you know Ashley."

"Your mother has a point, Cindy. We'd feel better about this if we could talk to Ashley's parents first."

"Okay," she said. Cindy knew when to give in. "I'll go call her."

The phone rang three times before a crisp voice said, "Hello."

"Hi, this is Cindy Lewis. May I speak to Ashley?"

"Just a moment, please." In a few seconds the line was picked up again. "She'll be right with you," the voice said in a businesslike manner.

"Hi, Cindy. Can you go?" Ashley asked.

"I think so But my mother wants to talk to your mother before everything's settled."

"Well, if your mom's home now, my mother's right here."

"Okay. Let me go get her." Cindy covered the receiver and hollered, "Hey, Mom, Ashley's mother's on the phone."

Cindy followed her mother back into the kitchen where she listened to one side of the conversation. After some small talk with Mrs. Corbett and a few jokes about raising teen-aged girls, Mrs. Lewis said good-bye. She then handed the phone back to Cindy. "Ashley wants to talk to you, dear."

"Well?" Ashley said.

"I think it's a yes. I'll call you back later."

"Okay. Oh, Cindy, I can't wait! It'll be so much fun."

Cindy wet back into the den. "Well?"

"I can meet Mrs. Corbett when she comes to pick you up. Your father and I agree—it sounds like a fun weekend."

Cindy let out a whoop of joy and threw her arms around her father's neck. "Thanks, Dad." She went over to her mother and gave her a quick hug. "You, too, Mom."

Chapter 6

*S*aturday morning *Mollie came into the kitchen* feeling restless. It was just past ten, and she was already bored. She thought of Cindy at San Simeon and wondered if it was cloudy there as well. Nicole was sitting at the counter eating a croissant and reading some French fashion magazine. *"Bonjour,"* Nicole said, looking up as Mollie came in.

"Bonjour," Mollie answered without much feeling.

"You want a croissant?" Nicole asked.

"Might as well." Mollie sighed. "There's nothing else to do. Where is everybody?"

"Well, Cindy's already gone, Mom is catering a wedding reception, and Dad is playing golf. Winston is lying in the garage pouting because Cindy didn't take him running today, and the cats were on my bed last time I checked."

"Oh." She got a glass and poured herself some milk to go with the croissant.

Mollie sat at the counter and wondered what she would do with herself all day. Everyone she called before coming downstairs this morning was busy doing something else. She had hoped to find someone who would go to the mall with her so she could see Greg again. She had stopped off to see him Thursday on the way home from school, but he wasn't in the pet shop.

"Hey, Nicole, you want to do something together?"

"Sorry, I can't. I already have plans."

"Oh." Mollie dropped her chin into her hand and thought of the long, dreary day ahead of her.

"Why don't you go play with Winston? He looks about as sad as you do today?"

Suddenly Mollie perked up. She would take Winston on a walk down the beach. She might even run into Greg. If not, it was impossible to stay unhappy around Winston. She jumped up and set her half-eaten breakfast on the counter.

"Aren't you going to finish that?" Nicole asked.

"Not hungry. Thanks for the idea, though." Mollie gave her beautiful oldest sister a big smile.

"What idea?"

"Never mind," Mollie yelled as she bounced out of the room. "Just thanks." She ran upstairs and was pulling clothes from the bottom of her closet and tossing them out onto her bedroom floor. She knew she had those cute red warm-up pants in there someplace. Ah, she thought, sitting back on her heels, there they were. She pulled them out from under her schoolbag.

Mollie stood up and shook them out. She pulled on an oversized T-shirt that was red-and-white, then brushed her long blond curls into a ponytail. She topped the ponytail with a big red ribbon. She leaned into the mirror and tried out the new eye-makeup technique she'd used on Sarah at the mall last week.

She gave herself a quick inspection in the mirror and decided she looked cute enough to go out. In the garage Mollie pushed the button that controlled the automatic garage door opened. It slid up, and Winston perked up his ears. "Come on, boy. Let's go for a walk."

Winston got to his feet and wagged his tail. He jumped around with excitement as he followed Mollie outside. He had given up on a walk for today.

"Now you stay with me," Mollie warned him, heading down to the beach. "I don't want to have to go tearing down the beach to catch you or anything." There weren't many people on the beach, and Mollie saw no signs of Greg. It was cool and overcast and looked like rain. The storm had kicked up some strong surf.

She and Winston walked along the water's edge. Winston wanted to take off running as he usually did with Cindy, but Mollie walked aimlessly along while staring out at the gray, rolling sea. Winston stopped and played in the water as he usually did. Mollie stopped impatiently and put her hand on her hip. "Winston. What are you doing?"

He picked up a stick with seaweed hanging from one end and ran after her. He nudged her leg to see if she was up for a game of catch, then dropped the stick at her feet. Mollie reached down, picked up the stick between two fingers, and tossed it toward the water. Winston raced toward the water and retrieved the stick and brought it back to Mollie again.

"Oh, Winston, you goofy dog," she said with a laugh. He bounded happily around her and waited for her to toss the stick again. "Okay, one more time." She threw the stick out to the water's edge. Winston dashed out and overran the stick. He made a clumsy stop and spun around looking for the stick. He found it and dashed happily back to Mollie.

She forgot all about "one more time" and was having as much fun as Winston. When her sore arm cried out for relief, she told Winston, "Enough, boy. We'd better be getting back anyway before the sky opens up and we get soaked." Dark clouds had begun rolling in and stacking up, and it felt as if it might pour any second.

Mollie felt more relaxed when she and Winston came into the garage. Walking him was fun. She'd have to start doing it more often—and she might even run next time! She bounced in the back door and found a new *Seventeen* in the mail pile. Eager to check out the new issue, she went upstairs to her room and read.

An hour later, when the phone rang, Mollie had already made a mental shopping list of the new clothes she wanted. Tearing herself away from a juicy article on attracting older boys, she ran down the hall to answer the phone.

"Mollie? It's Heather. What's going on?"

"Nothing much. I was reading the new *Seventeen*. Did yours come today?"

"Nope, not yet. Do you want to go to the mall? My mom has to do some shopping, and she'll give us a ride over there."

Mollie brightened. The threat of a long, dull day had certainly vanished, and she said, "When do you want to go?"

"In about half an hour."

"I'll be ready." She hung up the phone and zipped into her room to find something to wear. It would have to look great. She'd missed Greg at the beach, but maybe she would run into him at the mall. Mollie flipped through her clothes and finally settled on a royal-blue jumpsuit. She took the elastic band from her hair and let it fall. She'd need to use the electric curlers to put some spring back that the damp sea air took from it.

Thirty-five minutes later, Heather's mom pulled up out front and honked. Mollie taped the note she'd written for her mother to the refrigerator.

While driving through the parking lot at the mall, Heather's mother said, "I only plan to stay an hour and a half, so please don't keep me waiting!"

"We won't," Heather promised. Her mother had

barely rolled to a stop before the girls had the door open. "We'll see you back here then," Heather said. When they were away from the car, Heather asked, "What should we do first?"

"Go to the pet store."

"Okay, that'll be fun."

"You bet it will. There's this gorgeous guy working there, and I can't wait for you to see him." They went directly to the second floor and into the pet store. Mollie quickly scanned the store, but Greg wasn't there. She went to watch the puppies while she waited to see if Greg would come out of the back room.

Finally Heather went to the clerk behind the register and asked, "Is Greg working today?"

Mollie was mortified at first, then she heard the lady say, "He's on break. He should be back in about fifteen minutes."

Mollie's hopes plummeted. Heather came over to her and said, "Why don't we go get something to drink and come back in a little while."

"But that's no good, he'll know I came back just to see him," Mollie said.

"So what? It can't hurt if he knows you're interested. What have you got to lose? Come on, if we get going, we'll have time before we have to meet my mom."

They went to the center of the mall, where all the fast-food restaurants were surrounded by a bunch of tables. The girls got diet sodas and went over to sit down.

"Mollie, right?" Mollie turned around and saw

Greg standing next to the table. "Greg Masters. I work at the pet store, remember?"

"Sure! You want to sit down?" Mollie asked, fairly bursting with excitement.

He looked at his watch. "Well, I only have about five minutes left on my break, but I can sit down for a minute." He pulled a chair over and sat down. Heather cleared her throat.

"Oh, this is my friend Heather."

"Hi." He smiled at her politely before turning his attention back to Mollie. "I didn't see you on the beach this week."

"Well, I've been really busy. I didn't get out today until almost ten-thirty."

"With school every day and work every night, if I don't run early, I don't get to run at all. You must not have a job, huh?"

"A job?" He must have thought she was sixteen. She couldn't tell him she was only a freshman. And she felt like she needed to say something worthwhile to keep his interest.

"I'm sort of self-employed."

"Oh, really?" He looked at her with an amused smile. "How does someone as young as you become self-employed? Baby-sitting?"

"Well, something like that. I um ..." Remembering how much Greg liked animals gave Mollie an idea. "I take care of dogs. You know, walk them, dog-sit, stuff like that."

"Really?" he said, his interest picking up. "That's great. We're sort of in related fields then. I sell them, and you take care of them."

"Yeah."

"Do you do any grooming?"

"No. Mostly I just watch them."

"Is there much money in that?"

"Well, actually I'm just getting started." Heather was staring at Mollie with surprise in her eyes. This was the first she had heard of Mollie's business plans.

"Well, let me know how it goes. Keep in touch, why don't you?" He pushed his chair back. "I have to get back to work. Nice to meet you, Heather."

"Oh, Mollie, he's so cute," Heather gushed as he blended into the crowd of people and disappeared.

"Didn't I tell you?"

"But what was all that junk about starting your own business?"

"It wasn't junk," Mollie said. "I just thought it up, but it would be great to have my own money and be able to buy things I want." The more she talked about it, the better the idea sounded. She could hardly wait to get home and talk it over with her parents.

When Heather's mother dropped her off, Mollie hurried into the house. "Anybody home?" she called as she came through the door.

"We're in," her dad answered from the kitchen.

"How was the mall?" her mom asked.

"Okay. Guess what?"

"What?"

"I've decided to start my own business."

Mr. Lewis gave his wife an amused smile. "Oh, you have, have you?"

"What sort of business?" Mrs. Lewis asked.

"Dog-sitting."

"What?" they said in unison.

"You know. A baby-sitting service for dogs. Feeding them, walking them, stuff like that."

"Does this include using our house?"

"Well, only sometimes."

"And what about Winston and the cats?" her father said. "Have you given that any thought?"

She hadn't, of course. She hadn't given much thought to any of the details. "I think there's merit to your idea," Mrs. Lewis said, "but I think you have a few details to iron out."

"Like how you'll get your customers," her mother said.

"I'll advertise, like you do for Movable Feasts."

"That's expensive," Mrs. Lewis said. "It would take a big bite out of your profits."

"How about flyers?" Mr. Lewis suggested. "If you draw it yourself, we could run off copies inexpensively."

"Yeah, that's a great idea. I'll get started on it right away."

"Just remember, young lady. No animals in this house that are too big to keep in your room. We have enough confusion around here. We don't need to start a zoo, too!"

Chapter 7

*M*ollie had been right about the weather in San Simeon. Cindy watched the crashing waves slap the wall of rocks and shoot a spiral fan of water high into the air. The rain was falling only in a soft drizzle now. From time to time, however, it would really pour down.

Ashley came out of the bathroom. "Still raining?"

"Uh-huh," Cindy answered.

"Not much of a weekend for sun and surf."

"I'm glad I left my board at home," Cindy said, getting to her feet. "I don't think there's a graceful way to glide into the rocks out there, anyway. You ready?"

Cindy had been up over an hour waiting for Ashley to wake up. She had gotten silently out of bed and gone to the rocky cliffs to watch the storm on the ocean. There was something fascinating about watching a storm that was creating havoc just a few feet away from you while you stood safely on the rocks. She had come back to the room at seven-thirty and grabbed a quick shower. Finally, at 8:10, Cindy had woken up Ashley, and they were finally going to breakfast.

Mr. and Mrs. Corbett were just leaving the restaurant as the girls came in. "Do hurry, dear," Mrs. Corbett said in her crisp cool voice. "We want to leave here by nine-fifteen. Our tour is scheduled for ten, and you know how your father hates being late."

"Okay," Ashley said. Cindy had noticed how subdued she was around her parents, almost like a different person. She was glad they had missed having breakfast with them.

"Good morning, Cindy," Mrs. Corbett said. Cindy said hello, and Mr. Corbett nodded politely in her direction. Cindy had the feeling he didn't really like kids.

They stepped out under the awning, and Mrs. Corbett struggled with her pop-up umbrella, which wasn't popping up at the moment. "Can I help you with that?" Cindy asked.

Mrs. Corbett handed it to her. "Thank you, dear." She had called Cindy dear most of the trip. Cindy thought she might have trouble with names. But it was still better than Mr. Corbett, who still called her Sandy half the time.

Cindy was starving. She ordered pancakes, eggs, and sausage. Ashley said, "I can't believe how you can eat. I wish I could eat like that."

"Why don't you?"

"Are you kidding? I'd end up looking like the Goodyear blimp."

"Exercise like I do. You can eat all you want that way."

"I'd never make it. I'm not that disciplined. There wouldn't be enough hours in the day to work off everything I'd like to eat. Then again, the way my mother cooks, it's not that hard to diet!"

Cindy thought for a moment about Ashley's mother. She gave out about as much warmth as a deep freeze. Cindy had yet to see her really smile about anything.

All the say to San Simeon, Mrs. Corbett didn't want the girls to talk above a whisper. If Cindy would get enthusiastic about something she saw or start singing the song on her Walkman, Mrs. Corbett would glance over her seat long enough to let her know she was being a bother. Ashley said it made her mother nervous to have noise in the car when she was driving.

Things didn't pick up much when Ashley's father joined them. Mr. and Mrs. Corbett were both extremely civlized. In fact, they were so civilized they hardly ever talked to each other, much less to Cindy and Ashley.

Cindy couldn't help comparing this trip to ones she'd taken with her own family where they packed everything, including the dog, into their station wagon and headed off down the road singing and bickering and laughing and loving every minute of the trip together. This ride had been about as much fun as biting her tongue.

The Corbetts were waiting for the girls by the car as they came out of the coffee shop after breakfast. Mrs. Corbett was standing safely beneath her oversized umbrella. Mr. Corbett was pacing by the side of the car. Mr. Corbett unlocked the doors and got in the car. Cindy looked at her watch. It was exactly nine-fifteen

Hearst Castle was a mansion built by William Randolph Hearst in the early 1900s. It was an elaborate mansion where Hearst threw parties for guests that ranged from famous movie stars to European royalty. Cindy had heard about it before, but this was the first time she'd ever been there.

The ride up the steep winding hill to the mansion was a thriller. The bus wobbled around the turns, and Cindy tried not to smile at the expression of horror on Mrs. Corbett's face. She didn't look at all certain that they would make it to the top. Every once in a while, Cindy would look over the steep cliffs below and follow the grassy slope of the deep drop. It gave her chills.

The tour began with a walking tour of the outside grounds and the beautiful outdoor pool that was almost large enough to surf in. Cindy and Ashley broke free of the Corbetts. On the second stop of the tour, Ashley spotted two teen-age boys that were more appealing to her than anything the mansion had to offer. She pointed them out to Cindy.

"Aren't they cute?" she asked.

Cindy shrugged noncommittally. "They're all right, I guess."

"They must have been at the front of the bus," Ashley said, standing on her toes to get a better look at them. "I don't remember seeing them on the way up, do you?"

"I wasn't really looking," Cindy said.

Ashley managed to work her way little by little toward the area where the boys were standing. Each time they would walk to a different area of the tour, Ashley moved a little closer to the boys.

They neared the end of the tour, and Cindy knelt down to stare at the reflecting pool. It was designed so that when you got to ground level, it was perfectly geometric. If you took a picture from the right angle, it was almost impossible to tell which were the real statues and which were the reflections.

Suddenly someone stepped in behind her. Cindy noticed his reflection standing over her and turned around. "Hi," he said. "I saw you at the hotel earlier this morning. Where are you from?"

"Santa Barbara." Cindy stood up and looked around for Ashley.

"We're from San Diego."

"That's nice," Cindy said. "Excuse me." She started walking toward the bus. He fell into step beside her. Ashley was talking to the other boy outside near the bus.

"By the way, my name's Jim Monroe." They went over to where Ashley and the other boy were talking. Jim leaned casually against the back of the bus and rested his foot against the side. "So what's your name?"

"Cindy. Cindy Lewis." The four of them stood and talked for a few minutes until the rest of the people filtered out and onto the bus. Cindy slipped into a seat at the back of the bus. Much to her surprise, Ashley sat across the aisle from her and left Jim to sit beside her.

Ashley's parents were the last ones to get on the bus. "My dad must have wanted a good picture of the reflecting pool," she said. "He probably waited until everyone else had left so it would be just right. He's kind of a perfectionist." That was an understatement, Cindy thought.

On the way back to San Simeon, Ahsley and Neal seemed to be hitting it off very well. Cindy and Jim exchanged polite conversation. He was a nice guy, but Cindy had a nagging little feeling she didn't like. It was almost like she was being disloyal to Grant. It made her uneasy. She would be anxious to get back to the hotel and ditch these guys.

The coversation turned to surfing, and Ashley said, "Oh, Cindy's a great surfer. She's got trophies to prove it and everything."

"No kidding," Jim said, looking at her with renewed interest. "What contests have you won?"

"Mainly local stuff," Cindy said. "Nothing big."

"She's just being modest. Her room is full of trophies."

"Cut it out, Ash," Cindy said with an edge of annoyance to her voice. "Enough."

"Sure." Ashley couldn't see why Cindy always got so embarrassed about being good at something. Cindy watched the rain fall through the bus window. This weekend was sure turning out to be a big mistake.

Back at the hotel, Cindy waited impatiently for Ashley to ditch the boys. Finally she said, "I'll meet you in the room."

Cindy turned on the TV and lay across the bed. She was restless. She wanted to go jogging on the beach or even browse through the shops. Something. Anything to kill the monotony of just sitting around. She dozed off and woke up when she heard the door being unlocked. She sat up on the bed.

"You shouldn't have taken off so soon. They're really nice guys. They're planning a trip to Canada this summer. Doesn't that sound like fun?"

"Yeah." Cindy rolled off the bed and got to her feet. "You want to go for a walk or something?"

"I guess." Ashley looked out at the restless sea. "Those waves look pretty scary to me."

"We're just going to look at them, Ash, not go for a swim." Cindy grabbed her jacket. "Coming?" Ashley got her own jacket off the chair and followed Cindy out into the rain.

Just before dinner, the Corbetts called to say they were having dinner at the restaurant in town, and the girls could join them or go out on their own. Ashley jumped at the chance to be alone, and Cindy was relieved. After the first night they had all spent together, she wasn't anxious to have another fun-filled evening with the jolly old Corbetts.

Ashley took forever to get ready. Cindy was starving. She was pacing the room asking Ashley how much longer she would be.

"Relax," Ashley said. "Why don't you get changed?"

Cindy looked down at her jeans and hooded sweatshirt. "Why? What's wrong with this?"

"I just thought it might be damp after the walk along the ocean this afternoon."

"I hung it over a chair. It's dry."

"Well, I'll be through in here in a minute, and you can do your hair and put on some makeup."

"What for?"

"Don't you want to freshen up?"

"I'm fine," Cindy said. "Except I'm starving."

"Okay. Okay. I'm almost ready." Ashley came out of the bathroom a few minutes later wearing navy slacks and a new navy-white-gray-and-red angora sweater. "Ready?" she asked.

"I thought we were eating in the coffee shop."

"We are." She looked at Cindy, then down at the sweater she was wearing. "Well, this is all I have that's dry."

On the way to the coffee shop, Ashley seemed to be checking for something. The whole time they waited for the waitress and placed their order, Ashley kept looking around the restaurant. Cindy asked her what she was looking for, and

Ashley said nothing. Cindy assumed Ashley must have been worrying her parents would show up and ruin the evening. That was probably why she had dressed up—just in case they ran into them later that evening.

Then Ashley suddenly ducked behind her menu and began to study it. Cindy looked up just in time to see Neal and Jim stop at their table. "Hi," Neal said.

"Hi," Ashley said and smiled sweetly as she twirled a long dark curl around her finger.

"Mind if we join you?" Neal asked as he sat down next to Ashley. Cindy slid over worldessly and Jim sat down. Cindy saw the setup and understood why Ashley had spent so much time getting ready. And why she had suggested Cindy change her clothes and fix her hair. Well, Ashley could just forget it. Grant was the only guy she wanted to impress.

After they finished dinner, Neal said, "Hey, you guys want to walk over to the gift shop?"

"We went there this afternoon," Cindy said flatly.

"But I bet you didn't have ice cream, did you? They make terrific homemade ice cram," Jim said.

"That sounds good, doesn't it, Cindy?"

Cindy had to admit it sounded great. She loved ice cream. "Okay, I guess it sounds okay."

As they walked, Neal and Ashley paired off and straggled behind her and Jim. "Ashley says you're quite a swimmer." Jim said.

"I enjoy it," Cindy said.

"That's great. I love sports. I play baseball."

"Do you? I'm a real big Dodgers fan. You're from San Diego. Are you a Padres fan?"

"Yeah, actually my dad used to play for the Padres. Now he's a coach. He had my brother and me out swinging a bat almost before we could walk. It paid off, though. My brother's on a free ride at San Diego State."

"Your dad must be very proud."

"Oh, yeah, I guess he is. The funny thing about my dad is, he never says a whole lot one way or another. When I strike out, he says, 'Well, you've got the next game to do better.' If I hit a home run, it's 'That's great, Jimbo, but don't expect to do it every time.' I guess that's why he's such a good coach. He's real even-keeled."

They were at the gift shop, and Jim held the door for the rest of them. Cindy went to the case looking all the different flavors over closely. She finally settled on peanut-butter swirl.

The boys invited them back to their room, and Cindy said, "No, thanks," while Ashely said, "That sounds like fun."

"There's a great movie on HBO," Neal volunteered.

"I'm really beat," Cindy said.

"But it's only eight-thirty," Neal protested.

"I get up early to run." Cindy peeled off and started toward their room. Ashley came up behind her and took her by the arm.

"Come on, Cindy. It's just for a little while ... till the movie's over. Neal seems like a nice guy, but I wouldn't dare go to his room unless you come, too." Cindy didn't answer. "Please."

Well, it was Ashley's trip. Cindy wouldn't even be here if it weren't for Ashley. What was one night? "Okay, but just until the movie's over."

"Oh, Cindy, you're a pal."

Cindy and Jim sat on the floor and watched the movie while Ashley and Neal talked. Cindy got to her feet when the movie credits started to roll. 'You ready?" she asked. "We have to meet your parents at seven in the morning."

"Don't remind me," Ashley said, getting reluctantly to her feet.

"Do you really have to go so soon?" Neal asked. He grabbed her hand.

"I guess we better."

"Okay, then let me walk you to your room." He put his arm around her shoulders. "You coming, Jim?"

"No, don't bother," Cindy said quickly. "You don't need to put your shoes on.'

Jim settled back. "If you're sure."

"I'm sure," Cindy said. "It was nice meeting you." Ashley and Neal followed Cindy out hand in hand. She unlocked the door and said to Ashley, "I'll see you inside."

Half an hour later, Ashley drifted into the room and leaned against the door, a dreamy look in her eyes. "I'm in love." She sighed.

"Yeah, well, I'm in bed," Cindy answered. "Go to sleep."

The next day was a rip-roaring tour of the countryside with Mr. and Mrs. Personality. Cindy wondered if they ever had any fun.

She was never so glad to see anything as the red tile roof of her house when they finally turned into the driveway. Winston padded out to meet her, and Cindy dropped to one knee and affectionately rubbed his big furry head.

Cindy's parents came out when they heard the car out front. Cindy stood up, and her father surrounded her in a warm embrace. "How was the trip?"

"Good," Cindy said. Mr. Corbett popped the automatic trunk, and Cindy reached in for her bag. Mr. Corbett stepped out of the car. "Dad, Mom, this is Mr. Corbett."

"Robert," Mr. Corbett said. Her father and Mr. Corbett shook hands. He pointed to the car. "This is my wife, Karen." Mrs. Corbett leaned toward the open door and smiled.

Cindy's mom bent down and said, "We want to thank you for taking Cindy along. I'm sure she had a wonderful time." She stood up and put her arm around Cindy.

"Yes, thank you for everything, Mr. and Mrs. Corbett," Cindy added.

"You're welcome anytime, dear," Mrs. Corbett said with the same enthusiasm she'd shown all week.

"We enjoy taking Ashley's little friends along. It gives them both something to do," Mr. Corbett added. Cindy watched Ashley slump down in the backseat. "We'll ask Cindy again one day."

And I hope I'm busy, Cindy thought to herself. She stood between her parents, feeling the security and love they offered and thought of poor Ashley and her cold life with Mr. and Mrs. Corbett.

Chapter 8

"*H*ey, good-looking, what's your hurry?" Cindy felt Grant's arms around her waist and turned to see his smiling face.

"Miss me?"

"You bet," Grant said and gave her a quick kiss on the cheek. "I'm not letting you out of my sight for a whole weekend ever again. This place is dead without you."

They went into the cafeteria where the rest of the gang was waiting for the first-period bell to ring. Duffy stood up and waved his arms like a cowboy with a rope in his hand. Cindy laughed. "With that bright red hair, does he really think that he's that hard to spot?"

They moved through the usual obstacle course of tables and chairs to reach Duffy, Carey, and Anna. "How was the trip?" Duffy asked.

"She had a miserable time," Grant answered. "It rained and she left me behind, so there wasn't a drop of sunshine in her life."

"Oh," Duffy moaned. "That's bad, MacPhearson."

"Well, bad, yes. But partly true," Cindy said. "It *did* rain."

"And speaking of weekends," Grant said. "Guess who's going to be here this weekend?"

"Who?" Cindy asked.

"Trent."

"Trent who?" Duffy asked.

"Trent, one of Grant's best friends from Hawaii," Cindy said.

"Yeah, we grew up together. We just about cut our teeth on the same surfboard. And he's flying in this Friday afternoon. His spring break is next week, and he's coming out. He called yesterday afternoon."

"That's great. I can hardly wait to meet him."

"Yeah," Carey said. "Cindy will be great, Grant. She has a real knack for taking newcomers under her wing."

Cindy looked at Carey in surprise. "What do you mean by that?"

"Well, Ashley's keeping you so busy these days, you hardly have time for any of your old friends."

"I just want her to feel at home, that's all."

"Well, whatever," Carey said with a shrug. The bell rang, and she and Anna got up to leave. "See you guys at lunch," Carey said.

Grant stood up, too. "I've got to run." He squeezed Cindy's hand. "See you at lunch."

Cindy watched him go, then she turned to Duffy. "What did Carey mean by that crack about being too busy for my old friends?"

"Well, Carey *does* kind of have a point. How much have we seen of you since Ashley came into the picture?" Duffy asked.

"I've seen you guys."

"Sometimes. And tell me something else. How much time have you and Grant had together?"

Cindy thought about it. There had been that one night on the beach. And then ... "Just don't desert the rest of us," Duffy reminded her. "We miss you. Maybe it's time good ole Ashley found a guy of her own and gave you and Grant a little breathing room. That's all." Duffy looped his arm around her neck and pulled her toward him in a half-hearted hug. "See you at lunch."

Coming down the hall later that morning, Cindy saw Grant fiddling with the combination of his lock. From the look on his face, it was sticking again. "Move over and let an expert try it," Cindy said, nudging him.

"Be my guest," he said, stepping aside.

Cindy whirled the black dial and stopped at the numbers of his combination. She pulled easily on the lock and was surprised when it held firm. Grant laughed. "See?"

"Let me try again." Cindy concentrated more carefully on the next try, and still the lock stubbornly refused to open. "Would you like to borrow a book?" she asked with a smile.

On the way to her locker, Cindy said, "Grant, I've been thinking about something Duffy said. About how Ashley is just lonely, and that's why she feels like we always have to go everywhere together. I was thinking about your friend Trent."

"What about him?" Grant asked, playing dumb.

"Well, do you think we could fix them up?" It would be great. We could double, and it would be lots of fun."

"I don't know, Cindy. I hate to throw him into this without asking him first. And maybe Ashley would like to have something to say about all this."

Cindy handed Grant her American Lit book. "Wait'll you meet him on Friday. Then you can decide for yourself if you think they'd hit it off."

"But what about you?" Cindy asked.

"What about me?"

"Well, do you mind? Maybe the two of you would rather be alone to talk over old memories. We could go out together Saturday."

"I'd rather make new ones with you," he said with a wink.

"That's real nice of you. Your friend comes all the way from Hawaii to see you, and you expect him to want to hang around with me?"

"He will when he sees you."

"Well, maybe. But think about Trent and Ashley, okay? I think it would be fun."

Mollie sat at the table that afternoon studying the design she'd come up with for the flyers she planned to distribute around the neighborhoods and put up on the bulletin boards in various grocery stores. She'd come up with the name Movable Beasts, but one look from her mother killed that idea. Instead it was Mother's Pet service.

She decided to make the lettering bolder. She took the cap from a black magic marker and began to work. Her tongue darted out the corner of her mouth as she concentrated on her work.

Nicole came in the back door. The sound of the door slamming made Mollie jump, and she made a dark line on the page. "Ohhh," she whined.

"What's wrong?" Nicole asked.

"Look what you made me do?"

"Me? I just got here," Nicole reached out and took the page from Mollie. "Let me see that." She studied it carefully. "Hey, that looks great."

"You really think so?"

"Sure. What are you going to do with these?"

"Dad's going to run them off for me at the office and I'm planning to put them up all over the neighborhood."

"Then we'd better get rid of this," Nicole said. She took some liquid paper and dabbed it lightly over the black mark. "Good as new," she said with a smile.

Thursday evening Mollie was lost in her favorite show, *Family Ties,* when her mother called, "Mollie, you have a phone call."

Mollie, hoping it might be someone exciting like Greg, went into the kitchen to answer the phone. Never mind that Greg didn't have her phone number and there were a ton of Lewises in the Santa Barbara phonebook. He might have tried every one of them until he'd tracked her down. On that romantic notion, she said, "Hello," in her most sultry voice.

"Is this Mollie? The girl who put the flyer up at the supermarket about dog-sitting?" an elderly voice asked.

"Yes, it is," Mollie said, standing a little straighter and becoming more businesslike.

"I have a small poodle, Snowball," she said with affection. "I am interesting in finding some-one to care for her this Saturday. I'm going to San Diego with a friend, and I usually take her every-where I go, but my friend says she's allergic to dogs, even poodles, if you can imagine that. And anyway, I hate the thought of leaving her home alone all day, and I absolutely refuse to have her in some awful kennel. When I saw your flyer, I hoped you might be the solution to my problem."

While Molly was excited at the thought of the money she could earn, a little dog meant she wouldn't get to go to the mall, and she wouldn't get to see Greg. "What time would you need me?" Mollie asked.

"Not so fast, young lady. I would have to meet you first. I wouldn't leave Snowball with just anybody."

"Okay."

"Could you come by the house tomorrow after

school? You can meet Snowball. She's a good judge of character. We'll see how the two of you get along."

Mollie clutched the address the lady had given on the phone the day before as she walked along Magnolia, looking for 3417. The house was immaculately manicured. The shrubs were all evenly trimmed, and the lawn was as smooth as a golf green. Mollie followed the curved sidewalk to the front door, where she rang the bell. An attractive lady in her sixties answered the door. "You must be Mollie," she said. "Come in. I'm Mrs. Wallingford."

Mollie followed her into a sitting room off to the left of the entry hall. The room looked like something out of the *House Beautiful* magazines she always looked through in the dentist's office. Mollie sat carefully on one of the rose-colored high-back chairs. She bent over to set her books on the floor in front of her because she wouldn't dare set anything on the leaded glass table at her side.

"Would you care for some refreshment?" Mrs. Wallingford asked.

"No, thank you," Mollie said. Actually, Mollie would have loved something to drink, but she had visions of knocking something over and ruining the Persian rug. It was a beautiful room, but Mollie couldn't wait to get out of it.

"Well, now," Mrs. Wallingford said, "why don't you tell me about your experience with animals?"

She settled in on the cream-colored sofa across from Mollie. The little rose-colored buds of the fabric picked up the color in the older lady's cheeks.

"Actually I'm just starting my business," Mollie said in her most professional voice. "But we have a dog and two cats at home. I take care of them."

"I see."

"And I love animals," Mollie said.

"Well, Snowball has a real knack for spotting an imposter," Mrs. Wallingford said. She got up and left the room. Mollie began to sweat. The dog would probably come racing into the room and rip her leg off.

Mrs. Wallingford reappeared with a small furry bundle in her arms. The little ball of fluff squirmed and yipped as she talked to it. She turned the dog so that it faced Mollie. Cupping its little face in her slender hand, and said, "This is Snowball. Snowy, this is Mollie."

Mollie reached up to touch the dog. She'd never seen a cleaner animal in her life. She shuddered to think of how Winston would crush this delicate little creature beneath one of his big clumsy paws in an instant.

"Would you like to hold her?" Mrs. Wallingford asked.

"Oh, yes." Mollie reached up for the dog. This would be easy. Anything this cute and cuddly would be fun to watch for an entire day. She could keep this little dog in her room all day without anyone objecting one bit.

The dog turned in her lap and began to lick Mollie's chin. Mollie laughed and took hold of the dog, lifting her high in the air. Snowball stared at Mollie with huge brown eyes.

Mrs. Wallingford smiled. "I can see the two of you will be great friends. That's such a relief to me. She doesn't take to just anyone, you know."

"Really?" Mollie was pleased.

"I was afraid I'd have to cancel my trip. I just couldn't leave her in a kennel for the day. All those other dirty animals barking and frightening her. That would never do. And then who knows what kind of dog might end up next to her? She could even—heaven forbid—get fleas! One must think of all the dangers...."

"Of course," Mollie agreed. She could see the dollar signs adding up already. This was going to be easy money.

Chapter 9

*G*rant had finally convinced Cindy to go out with him and Trent. Friday night when she heard Grant's car pull up, she grabbed her jacket, yelled, "See you later," and went out the door. Grant was coming up the walk and kissed her lightly. He slipped his arm around her and walked with her to the car. A tall, lanky boy with light brown hair, a great tan, and an infectious smile was leaning against the passenger door, his arms folded casually across his chest. He smiled and dimples creased the sides of his face. He was a doll. He would be perfect for Ashley.

He stood up and came forward. "So. This is Cindy."

"So. This is Trent," she answered.

"I see there's no need for introductions," Grant said with a shrug. They got into the car. Cindy couldn't help but notice how Trent's long legs were practically under his chin in the backseat of the Trans Am. "Why don't I ride back there and give you a little more room?" Cindy offered.

"Naw," he said. "I don't want to come between you two." He grinned up into the rearview mirror, and Grant looked back at him. Cindy didn't completely catch the look that passed between them.

"Besides, it's good for him to be uncomfortable now and then."

"And look at it this way," Trent continued. "At least I'll have something to hold tonight." He put his arms around his knees and Cindy laughed.

"Okay, if you're sure. But if you change your mind, we can trade places anytime."

They had a great time playing miniature golf and riding bumper boats. All three of them were still soaked when they came into Taco Rio. Duffy and Carey were there.

"Come on," Grant said. "There's someone I want you to meet." He led them over to Duffy's table. "Hi, everyone. This is Trent. Trent, meet Duffy and Carey."

"Is it raining?" Duffy asked, looking at their wet clothes.

"Bumper boats," Grant explained.

"I don't know about anyone else, but I'm starving," Trent said. "Come on, Cindy, help me decide what we're going to eat."

They ordered a large pizza, and when they had finished, Cindy went into the bathroom to clean up a little. The door opened, and Carey came in. "You still talking to me?" Carey asked.

"Sure." Cindy shrugged. "Why wouldn't I be?"

"Well, the other day I said some pretty sarcastic stuff. And well, I'm sorry."

"Hey, it's no biggie," Cindy said. She tossed the paper towel into the trash. "Two points," she said with a grin.

"I just want you to remember we're your friends, too."

"Carey, you know I'd never forget that." She opened the door. "Come on. Those guys'll wonder what we're doing in here."

Trent stayed in the car while Grant walked Cindy to the door. "Well, what do you think?"

"That you're terrific."

"No. I mean about Ashley and Trent."

"Well, ask her to meet us at the beach tomorrow. Let's see how they hit it off and take it from there."

"How'd you get so smart?"

"Hanging around with you, I guess." He leaned over to kiss her good night, and Trent blasted the horn of the car.

Cindy jerked up and the light came on out on the porch.

"Everything all right?" her mother asked, opening the door. "I thought I heard someone honking."

"Grant's ride is anxious to get home," Cindy said, patting his cheek. "See you tomorrow."

"If I'm not in jail for murder." He brushed her lips with his and rushed out to the car.

*   *   *

Cindy had just come in the back door from her
morning run when the doorbell rang. It was barely
seven-thirty. She opened the door to see a slightly
overweight older lady with silver hair. "Is this the
Lewis residence?" She was holding a basket
trimmed in lavender that was making suspicious
noises.

"Yes," Cindy answered.

"I'm looking for Mollie."

"Oh, you must be Mrs. Wallingford. I'm Mollie's
sister Cindy. Come on in. I'll get Mollie." She ran
up the stairs and beat on Mollie's door. Mollie
lifted the pillow from her head and rolled over.

"What do you want?" she asked sleepily.

"Your charge is here." Cindy closed the door
again, and Mollie sat up abruptly and looked at
the clock. It was already seven-thirty. How had
that happened? She had purposely set her alarm
for seven so she could be dressed and looking
presentable for Mrs. Wallingford when she brought
Snowball by. The last thing she had wanted was
for Mrs. Wallingford to meet a sweaty Cindy just
back from a run and form an impression about
her family based on that. Oh, why couldn't Nicole
have answered the door?

Mollie grabbed a robe and dashed downstairs
to meet Mrs. Wallingford. Snowball was in a basket that had been obviously made just for her.
The white wicker basket had a lid that flipped up
on either side. One end was open, and Snowball's
white curly head peeked out from the lavender-

lined basket trimmed in white lace and purple ribbon.

"Doesn't she look cute?" Mollie took the basket Mrs. Wallingford was holding. She also handed Mollie something that looked like a diaper bag made of the same fabric as the basket lining. "This is her food. She eats a quarter cup three times a day. She's already had her breakfast. She'll want lunch at noon. Remember, dear, only a quarter cup. And please, no table scraps. Her system is very delicate."

"Yes, ma'am."

"I should be back by seven or eight this evening." She leaned down and cupped the dog's face in her hands. "Bye, bye, lamb chop. Mommy wuves you." She kissed the dog on the tip of her nose and blew more kisses as she went out the door. Mollie closed the door.

"Well, I'm going to get dressed," she said.

"I'm going to throw up," Cindy replied, looking at Mollie and the dog.

Mollie took Snowball up to her room and set the basket on the floor while she began trying to find something to wear for the day. She was going to have to pick up her room someday soon. It was hard to believe she could find anything to wear in the clutter.

Mollie heard rustling and looked over at the basket. Snowball was gone. Mollie looked around, but she couldn't see the small white fur ball anywhere. She called her, and a small whine answered. Then she heard a rustling sound. Mollie lifted her quilt and tossed it in the middle of the unmade bed. "Ah-hah!" she cried, but the dog wasn't hiding under the quilt.

She got on her knees and looked under the bed. Snowball didn't seem to be under there either. But there was so much junk under her bed that it was impossible to tell for sure. She pulled a few boxes out and reached for a bundle that looked like Snowball. Instead of a poodle, Mollie pulled out the white stretch pants she had been searching for on Monday.

Mollie heard a sound in the closet behind her, and she scurried across the floor on her hands and knees and began pulling dirty clothes from the piles inside the closet. After carefully checking each item, she tossed it onto the bed. She called the dog's name as sweetly as she could. Finally a little brown nose popped out from inside one of her soft fleecy sweatshirts, and Mollie reached down gratefully and picked up the little dog, who was stuck inside the arm of the sweatshirt.

Mollie watched her more carefully after that for the next few hours. At lunchtime she went into the kitchen and got out the measuring cup. She took the Tupperware container Mrs. Wallingford had packed with the specially prepared dog food from the lavender bag. She got out one of her mother's good dishes. After all, she couldn't expect a dog like Snowball to eat off a filthy dog dish like Winston did.

Through the screen of the garage door, Winston paced and barked as he saw the small intruder walking freely in the kitchen of his house. He couldn't understand why he wasn't allowed inside today.

"You be good," Mollie scolded him. "Cindy's already taken you running today, and you've been fed." His ears drooped, and he tried one more bark to see if she might change her mind. Mollie walked over and shut the wooden door on him.

Snowball attacked the dog food in the delicate crystal ice cream dish. Mollie sat by and watched her eat, jumping at every noise. She wanted to get the dish washed and back in the cupboard before anyone got home and saw what she had done.

Mollie cuddled Snowball on her lap later that afternoon as she cried through the sad ending of an old movie on TV. Smokey and Cinders watched cautiously from across the room, unsure of whether or not to trust the strange fuzzy newcomer.

The phone rang and Mollie got up till wiping her eyes. She shifted the dog to the other hip and reached for the receiver.

"Mollie, it's Sarah."

"What's up?" Mollie asked. That's when Snowball began to squirm. Mollie set her down, and the dog began to jump in circles around her feet and bark in high piercing yelps.

"What's that sound?" Sarah asked.

"I'm dog-sitting today."

"You have a job already?" she asked. "That's great. I never thought it would work out when you were telling me about it at school the other day. Does Greg know you're working?"

"Not yet." Snowball was pulling on Mollie's pant leg. Mollie was trying to shake her free and still hear what Sarah was saying about the new boy in their math class.

"Just a minute," Mollie said. She set the phone down and took the dog in her arms. "Come on, Snowy, we're going out." Mollie opened the french doors to the backyard. She set the dog outside. For a minute the dog looked completely confused. Was this some new kind of game? Then Mollie closed the door, and she began to yip loudly. Mollie went back to the kitchen and took the phone. "Make it fast," she said "I can't leave her out there very long."

Thirty minutes later, Mollie went to the back door. There was no white poodle waiting anxiously to come in. She opened the door and went into the yard. "Snowball," Mollie called sweetly. "Come here, little girl. Come to Mollie." She saw movement in the bushes. "Come to Mollie."

A muddy brown mess squirmed out of the flower bed. Mollie screamed, and the dog dashed back into the bushes. Mollie dropped to her knees and called, "I'm sorry, girl. I didn't mean to scare you. Come on. Come here."

Snowball backed farther away. Mollie started crawling in after her. The wet mud squished into the knees of her pants. Her mother would die when she saw them. Mollie bent down and reached up under the bush. She could almost reach her.

Something caught her long hair and she screamed. Snowball retreated farther into the bushes.

"Ohhh," Mollie cried, sitting back on her heels. She felt the back of her hair and pulled loose a branch that was hanging there. The dog slowly began to creep forward, head bowed in shame. Mollie looked at the dirt-matted dog and thought she looked more like a mudpie than a snowball right now. Mrs. Wallingford would scream if she saw her like that.

Mollie took the dog and went into the house. She dashed upstairs and into the bathroom. She pulled open the cabinet and looked for something she could use to clean the dog. There wasn't any dog shampoo up there, and even if there were, she wouldn't dare use anything so harsh on Snowball.

Then Mollie spotted some baby shampoo. Between surfing and the swim team, Cindy was always washing her hair, so she used the gentlest shampoo around. If it was gentle enough for a baby, it shouldn't hurt Snowball.

Mollie set the dog in the white tub and began running water over her. Snowball shook violently while Mollie talked soothingly to her. Mollie poured some shampoo into her hand and lathered up the dog. She held the shaking fragile body under the warm spray of water. "Isn't this fun?" Mollie said. "I just love taking showers." Snowball shook violently from side to side, throwing out a spray of water. "Guess they're not your favorite thing."

She lifted the dog out and set her carefully on one of her mother's good towels. She wrapped the towel around the squirming poodle and rubbed vigorously. Leaving Snowball on the floor, Mollie turned around and reached for the blow dryer.

The motor whined to life, and Snowball barked loudly. Mollie turned abruptly and saw the door shut behind her as Snowball escaped down the hall. She pulled the cord out of the wall and the blow dryer went silent. She dropped the blow dryer and ran into the hallway.

Luckily, only her door was open. She went into her room to find Snowball huddled in a pile of clothes in the bottom of the closet. She carefully lifted the dog up.

"Come on, girl. Let's get you dry before you catch a chill." She shuddered to think what Mrs. Wallingford would do if she picked up her precious pup and was greeted with a sneeze right in her face.

Mollie went back into the bathroom with the dog and took the blow dryer off the floor. She turned it on and nothing happened. She saw it was unplugged and plugged it in before trying again. It began to blow a stream of hot air, then mysteriously died. Mollie shook it a few times only to have it start up, then stop again. She tried one last good shake and nothing happened.

Mollie unplugged it and put it back in the drawer. "Looks like we're stuck with towel drying this time." Mollie took a towel from the shelf. She rubbed energetically and vowed not to let the dog out of her sight for the rest of the day.

Chapter 10

*W*hile Mollie had chased Snowball around her room Saturday morning, Cindy was downstairs calling Ashley. Even though she was anxious to get to the beach, she waited until nine-thirty to call.

It was a perfect day for the beach The sky was clear and the waves were good. It would be ideal weather for Trent to try his luck in the California waters.

"Ashley," Cindy said when she heard Ashley's sleepy hello. "It's Cindy. Look, grab your best swimsuit and meet me at the beach in an hour. Grant has this cute friend here from Hawaii, and I want you two to meet each other."

"Really?" Ashley sat up in bed, no longer the least bit tired.

"Is he as cute as Grant?"

"Almost. Look, I'll bring food. Just get up and get to the beach as soon as you can."

As Cindy hung up the phone, Grant rang the doorbell. Cindy grabbed the basket of towels and cooler of food. "Where is everybody?" Grant asked when he stepped into the silent house.

"Well, Mollie's dog-sitting up in her room and my dad's at the golf course and Nicole's helping my mom with a wedding shower."

"Quite the busy house!"

"That's right. It's just you and me to get all this stuff loaded."

"Not quite," Grant said. "Hey, Trent, get in here and earn your keep." Trent climbed out of the car and came up to the door. He took one of the canvas bags from Cindy. The three of them piled everything into Grant's car.

When Grant had parked at the beach, Trent opened the door and go out. "This is almost as good as Hawaii," he said, looking at the breaking waves. He took the cooler of food from Cindy and followed Grant over to where Duffy and Jason were waxing the surfboards.

"Let's hit those waves, buddy," Trent said, setting the food down and slapping Grant on the back. "What are we waiting for?" Laughing and joking, the two of them paddled out into the cold water. Cindy stood on the shore and watched them go.

"Why aren't you going?" Duffy said, coming up to stand beside Cindy.

"I want to watch Trent in action first," Cindy

said. "Let's see if he's as good as Grant thinks he is."

"He probably wants to know the same thing about you," Duffy said. Cindy shaded her eyes and kept them trained on Trent. Both guys picked the same wave. They got to their feet and began moving toward the shore. Trent maneuvered himself expertly from side to side on the board. He really was almost as good as Grant. Together they coasted into the shore after their successful ride. Cindy went over to greet them.

"Your turn," Grant said.

"Yeah, let's see if you can *really* surf or if love has blinded my old buddy," Trent said.

"That's funny," Duffy said. "We were just talking about that."

"Come on, Duf," Cindy said.

"No, thanks. I'll wait this one out. It's all yours."

Cindy paddled out into the water and waited. She caught a good wave with lots of roll to it. She rose easily to her feet and began working her board toward the shore. She couldn't help but wonder what Trent thought of her. Then it happened. Fifty yards from shore, her board jumped out from under her. Cindy went flying awkwardly through the air, landing in the water with a huge splash. When she came up, she just snagged the corner of her board. Humiliated, she caught it and rode the rest of the way to shore. Cindy still didn't know what had happened. She did know one thing. She had just made a complete fool of herself in front of Grant, Trent, and all her friends.

"You're right," Trent said, laughing, "she is dynamite." He came into the shallow water near the edge of the ocean and reached for her board. "Are you okay?" he asked Cindy.

"Yeah, I'm fine," Cindy said, pulling her board away from him. She didn't mind wiping out, and Cindy had surfed long enough to know it could happen to anybody. But why did it have to happen in front of Trent?

"She's just being nice 'cause she didn't want to show you up your first day surfing here," Duffy said. "But watch out—now she'll knock you off your feet when you least expect it."

"That's what she did to me," Grant piped in. "But not just surfing." He put his arm around Cindy and walked with her toward the beach. "What happened?" he whispered.

"I don't know. I just lost it."

"Serves me right for bragging about how you beat the pants off me in that surfing contest. Why couldn't you have wiped out last fall and let me win?" He pulled her closer to him and gave her an affectionate squeeze.

"I think I'd have rather done it then," Cindy said with a smile.

Duffy tore open a bag of chips and began shoving some into his mouth. "Anybody else hungry?"

"I am," Jason said.

"Me, too. Wiping out always gives me an appetite."

"Hey." Carey laughed. "Don't blame that on the ocean."

They were taking the last of the hot dogs from the fire when Ashley got there. She came strolling across the sand in a white lace cover-up over a tiny bright red bikini. Her dark curly hair was pulled back in a ponytail tied with a red ribbon. Cindy noticed Trent's interest.

"Ashley," Cindy said. "About time you got here. You know everyone but Trent. He's a friend of Grant's from Hawaii."

"Hi, Trent. It's nice to meet you." Ashley extended one of her tiny hands toward him. Caught by surprise, Trent shoved the remainder of his hot dog into his mouth in order to have a free hand to shake hers. But then he found he couldn't say hello because his mouth was full. After a few seconds, he swallowed uncomfortably and finally managed to say hi.

Grant pulled Cindy off to the side. "Well, so far so good. Trent's usually not speechless." For the rest of the afternoon, however, Trent and Ashley found lots of things to talk about. From time to time, Cindy found herself watching Trent's animated face as he talked and Ashley laughed. Trent noticed her watching him and came over to her.

"Well, California girl, are you ready to teach this Hawaiian a thing or two?" He lifted his board from the sand.

"Like how to wipe out?" Cindy said.

"I already know that. Come on. I'll show you."

Cindy got her own board and followed him to the water's edge. The pounding waves had picked up considerably since earlier that morning.

They paddled out into the ocean. "You know," Trent told her, "I'm glad to see Grant happy here. He was really upset about having to move. He was really something special in Hawaii."

"He's special here, too."

"Yeah. I can see that. And so are you." He smiled at her. "Not many girls have kept Grant interested for more than a month or two. So I figure you must be pretty special."

"I am," she said with a confident wink. "Get up on that board of yours, and I'll show you."

They turned and positioned themselves and waited for the big one. Once Cindy was up, she concentrated only on having a good ride. She knew one fall wasn't a big deal, but she didn't want Trent to think she really couldn't surf.

Like the first one, this ride felt pretty routine. The ride should have been. The water had gotten rougher, but she'd ridden worse. Cindy pushed everything out of her mind but the natural feel she had for the water and the board beneath her feet. She glided into the shore with no problem.

Trent glided in beside her. "Now that's the kind of ride Grant told me you could make." He laughed and shook the water from his hair. "I guess you are pretty good." He put his arm casually across her shoulders. "For a California girl. One of these days you'll have to have Grant bring you to Hawaii and we'll show you some real waves."

"No, thanks," Cindy said, slipping easily from beneath his arm. "I'll just stay here and work with what I've got."

"You're right, MacPhearson," Trent said. "She is something else."

"Didn't I tell you?" Grant put his arm around Cindy. Cindy snuggled a little closer. This guy she didn't pull away from.

Chapter 11

*T*he next week passed, and Cindy didn't see much of Grant. He was anxious to show Trent all the highlights of Southern California. While Cindy missed him, and the week without him had really dragged along, she knew it was a good idea to spend some time with Duffy, Carey, and all her other friends. But now Cindy was upstairs in her room, hurrying to get ready. Grant was picking her up in thirty minutes to spend the day at Disneyland.

Trent was really getting the royal tour. Grant had even "gotten the flu" one day during the week so he and Trent could go on the Universal Studios tour. Universal was one of Hollywood's biggest moviemakers. Every day they offered tours of the big studio sound stages. Tourists could see where a lot of famous movies and TV shows were made.

Sometimes members of the tour group got to take part in a video taping of a short movie. Grant told Cindy that he and Trent volunteered to be bandits and had to jump into a tank of water. The studio then sold copies of the tape, and Trent had bought one to show all his friends back in Hawaii.

Ashley and Trent had been unable to work out a date until now because it seemed Ashley's parents always had other plans for her. It had finally worked out that they would all be able to spend the last day before Trent had to leave at Disneyland.

Cindy reached into her drawer and pulled out a pair of jeans. She went to her closet and got a polo shirt and matching sweater. The blue and lavender were good colors for her. She brushed her short blond curls and dabbed the tips of her long lashes with mascara. That was about as much as she ever used. She didn't like much makeup.

Cindy heard the doorbell ring and dashed down the stairs to answer it. Grant and Trent stepped in when she opened the door. Mr. and Mrs. Lewis came into the living room, and Cindy introduced everyone.

"You kids have a good time," Mr. Lewis said, walking them to the door. "And drive carefully. You have precious cargo there."

"Oh, Dad, cut it out," Cindy said with a hint of embarrassment. "We'll see you guys later tonight."

"No later than twelve," her mother reminded her before she closed the door.

"Nice family," Trent said.

"You didn't even see the best part," Cindy said. "She has two of the best-looking sisters in Santa Barbara."

"Well, let's go back," Trent said, vaulting over the car door and starting back up the walk.

"Whoa! You're already set for today. Remember?" Grant asked.

"Right. To Ashley's." As usual. Ahsley wasn't quite ready. At some point, Cindy was going to have to tell her how annoying that was. Finally Ashley came down the stairs in bright yellow shorts with a sleeveless oversized blouse of yellow, purple, and red plaid. Cindy had to admit with her dark hair and deep tan, she really looked good in yellow. Trent seemed almost mesmerized by her as she came down the stairs.

On the way to Disneyland, Trent said, "I've really been looking forward to this. I know it sounds kind of silly, since Disneyland is a kid's place. But when I was little, I watched *The Wonderful World of Disney* all the time."

"What's this when-I-was-a-kid stuff?" Grant asked. "You're still watching Disney, and you know it."

"Well, I love Disneyland," Ashley said. "We stopped there while we were on our way from Oregon. Our Santa Barbara house wasn't ready yet, so we stayed in a hotel for a few days. Disneyland's not exactly my dad's thing, but it sure beat sitting around that hotel for another day doing nothing. Even my parents enjoyed it.

And Cindy can tell you that's amazing." Cindy looked at her and grinned.

While Grant was parking the car, Cindy outlined their strategy. "We should ride the Matterhorn first. Then Space Mountain and Big Thunder. As the crowds get bigger, their lines get longer. Then we can see the less-crowded stuff later."

They all enjoyed the Matterhorn, which was a big roller coaster that ran around and through what looked like one of the Swiss Alps. However, Space Mountain was too much for Ashley. It was a roller coaster, too, but it spun and dropped through almost complete darkness.

Ashley walked unsteadily away from the ride, holding her stomach. "All that spinning in the dark got to me," she said. "I don't think I'm up for Big Thunder right now."

"Aw, come on," Trent said.

"Pirates of the Caribbean is on the way back to Big Thunder. Let's ride that and give our stomachs a rest," Cindy suggested.

"Okay, but then we go right over to Big Thunder, or Cindy and I are taking off without you guys." Trent put his arm around Cindy and gave her a quick hug.

"Why don't we all go later," Grant said with a trace of annoyance in his voice.

By lunchtime they had hit all the big rides and started back through the park again. They paddled canoes in Frontier Land and rode through the Safari and Mark Twain's Steamship. They

snacked some more and then went for a subma-
rine ride.

Finally they collapsed on a bench beneath a
shady tree. "This place is great," Trent said enthusiastically. "I could spend a week here. There's
so much to do!" Grant came back with ice cream
for everybody.

"Grant, old buddy," Trent said, "I can understand why you like living here. I never thought I'd
say this, but it's almost better than Hawaii. I
mean, you still have the ocean, but there's lots of
other stuff to do here, too. And you have other
attractions here we don't have back home." He
winked at Cindy. Grant instinctively tightened his
arm around her.

"Well, let's go," Cindy said, getting up. "Who's
up for another ride down Space Mountain?"

"Not me," Ashley said. "I know I'd get sick,
especially since we just ate."

"Me, too," Grant said. "I'm going to let things
settle a bit."

"Come on, Cindy," Trent said. He jumped to his
feet and took her hand. "I'll go with you." He was
pulling her toward the other side of the park
before she had time to protest.

"We'll meet you guys back here in half an hour,"
Cindy yelled over her shoulder. She thought that
would give them plenty of time to wait on line
and still make it back. But the lines were longer
than she expected, and it took almost forty minutes just to get on the ride. When they finally got

back to the bench where they were supposed to meet Grant and Ashley, no one was there.

"Where'd they go?" Trent asked, looking in all directions.

"Who knows? They probably went to look at something. I'm sure they'll be right back. We can wait here." Cindy sat on the bench.

"But what if they're out looking for us? We might sit here the rest of the day. I only have one day to spend here, and I don't want to spend the rest of it on this bench."

"We'll never find them in all these people. We'd better stay here."

"Okay. But if they're not back in thirty minutes, I say we forget about it and have some fun. We'll run into them eventually. And even if we don't, we can meet them at the car when it's time to leave."

Thirty minutes later there was still no sign of them. Trent was anxious to move on, and Cindy was a little ticked off at them for leaving at all. Grant should have known she'd come back. He should have waited for them. "Come on," Trent urged. "I may not get back here for years. We've wasted enough time sitting around here. Let's go."

Cindy looked around one last time. "Well, maybe we'll run into them soon," she said doubtfully. It was nearly three hours later when they stumbled into them.

Cindy had finally talked Trent into going on one of her favorite rides, It's a Small World.

"You'll love it," she promised. "It's a boat ride through a whole world of puppet shows. The puppets sing, and dance, and are dressed like people from all over the world."

"It sounds like a little kid's ride," Trent protested.

"Oh, come on, Trent! It's really cute, and a lot of fun," Cindy urged.

"Okay, but you have to promise to hold my hand if I get scared," Trent teased.

"Don't be a wimp." She pulled him toward the line of people. "Come on, we can get in the next boat."

When the boat started to move, Trent said, "Now remember, you promised to hold my hand."

Cindy took his hand. "There. Satisfied?"

Cindy heard a shout. "Cindy!" She sat up and tried to look around. "Over there." She tried standing up, but the boat started to sway. Trent pulled her back to her seat just as they went into the tunnel.

"That was Grant," Cindy said.

"What was?"

"Didn't you hear someone call me?"

"No."

"Well, I did." Cindy tried to look behind the boat, but it was no use. They were too far inside the tunnel, and there was nothing she could do about it now. Trent pointed to the puppets and sang along with the song and had more fun than he had thought he would. As they came out on the end of the tunnel, Trent squinted into the setting sun and said, "Hey, there's Grant and Ashley."

Cindy climbed out of the boat and ran over to Ashley and Grant. "Where'd you guys go?" Cindy said.

"Where'd *we* go?" We waited for an hour before we gave up on you! We didn't come here to spend the whole day sitting on a park bench. We tried to find you, but you must have taken off before we got there. We stood by the ride and watched people getting off for thirty minutes. Then we went back to the bench, and you guys weren't there either, so we decided to walk around and hope we'd run into you."

"Well, you did," Trent said. "Good work, buddy." He slapped Grant on the back.

Grant was very quiet for the rest of the day. When they stopped to drop off Ashley, and Trent was walking her to the door, he asked Cindy, "What did you guys do all afternoon?"

"What do you mean? Mostly we hunted for you."

"You didn't look like you were searching too hard when I saw you on the Small World ride."

"What are you getting at?" Before he could answer, Trent opened the door. Cindy leaned forward and he climbed into the backseat.

On the way to Cindy's house, the only one doing any talking was Trent. He eventually gave up after he tried to ask several questions and got only one-word replies.

Grant stopped the car at Cindy's house, and

she opened her door. Trent reached up and grabbed Cindy's arm. "Hey, get my address from Grant and write me sometimes. And if you can make it over to Hawaii one of these days, I'll show you some real surfing." He winked at her.

"Yeah, sure. I just bet you will. Hey, it's been fun. I enjoyed meeting you." Grant just about pulled Cindy out of the car. "What's your problem?" she asked.

"I don't want you writing him. The next thing you know, he'll be calling you, and you'll be taking off for Hawaii, and I'll never see you again."

"Aren't you being a little melodramatic? I live here, you know. We're bound to run into each other at school every now and then."

"You don't know Trent, Cindy. He's always determined to outdo me. If I buy a new surfboard, he gets a better one. If it's a new car, his is faster. And now he's after you, too."

"Grant, he's your best friend. And that's all he is to me. A friend. Okay? Just like Duffy."

"No. He's not like Duffy. I trust Duffy. Trent's another story. You think I don't know why he managed to get you two lost today?"

"We weren't lost. *You're* the ones who took off. Remember?"

"Yeah, but that was because I knew what he was doing. *He* was waiting all day for a chance to be alone with you."

'Yeah, well, you spent the afternoon with Ashley. So what?"

"Well, at least we weren't holding hands!" he snapped.

"Oh, so that's what's bothering you," Cindy said. "Come on, Grant, that was no big deal."

"Maybe not to you."

"If I saw you and Ash holding hands, I wouldn't get upset."

"That doesn't surprise me."

"Why?"

"Because I don't think you would have cared no matter what we did. I don't think you care enough about me to get jealous."

"That's crazy."

"Hey, MacPhearson," Trent yelled from the car, "are you coming?"

"In a minute," Grant yelled back. "Is it? You act like everybody is one big happy family. 'We're all just the best of friends here,' " Grant mocked sarcastically. "I've accepted you and Duffy—there's not much I can do about that. But I don't want to think that you're going to run around being best friends with every guy you meet."

"Why not? You can have all the *female* friends you want. That doesn't change how *we* feel about each other. I'm not going to tear somebody's hair out just because she talks to you or holds your hand on a stupid ride at Disneyland."

"Well, I am."

"Now I know why you like Disneyland so much, Grant," Cindy fumed. "Because you never bothered to grow up." The door slammed loudly behind her.

Chapter 12

"*It's been three days already! I still can't be-* lieve you're not going to call Grant," Mollie said when Cindy came into the kitchen that afternoon.

"Why should I? He keeps giving me dirty looks, and he doesn't have any reason to be mad."

"Here we go again." Mollie sighed. "It seems to me the last time you guys weren't talking to each other, you were both miserable but just too stubborn to admit it."

"We're still speaking," Cindy said.

"Barely." They heard a car horn out front.

"That must be Ashley's mom." Cindy was going to Ashley's to work on geometry. Cindy was still struggling, and Ashley seemed to grasp it pretty easily. Since the Corbetts were going out for the evening, Ashley had suggested they work at her house.

Things were so tense between Grant and her that Cindy actually found she was looking forward to studying. The diversion would take her mind off Grant for a while. Neither one of them had mentioned their argument, but it stood between them like an invisible wall. While she waited for his apology, he was probably waiting for hers.

They pulled up in front of the Corbett house. "We should be home about ten," Mrs. Corbett said. "I hope you get a lot of studying done. And don't mess up the house. We might bring people back after dinner."

Ashley closed the door and turned to Cindy. "I think it's about time you made some of those famous brownies I've heard so much about. I'll think better on a full stomach."

While Cindy mixed her secret brownie recipe, Ashley handed her ingredients and put things away. "You realize we'll have to eat all of those before my mother gets home, don't you?" she asked. "She'll die if she thinks we messed up her kitchen. I really think that's why she never cooks. She can't stand a mess." The more Cindy knew of the Corbetts, the more she realized Ashley wasn't kidding about a lot of the things she said about her family.

The girls sat down and opened their books. "Seen much of Grant this week?" Ashley said casually. "Is something wrong? Things haven't seemed right between you two since we went to Disneyland?"

"They're okay."

"That's good," Ashley said. "You should have seen him when we lost you two Saturday. By the way he was searching for you, you'd have thought you'd been kidnapped by Jack the Ripper."

Cindy winced. It was bad enough Grant had acted like a dope about things, but she hated to think he'd been so obvious about it. "Let's just get this geometry done, okay?" Cindy suggested.

"Sure," Ashley agreed. The buzzer sounded, and Cindy got up to check the brownies.

Two hours later, they closed their books and put the last of their dishes in the dishwasher. Cindy should have felt great. Thanks to Ashley, she'd finally understood the concept that had been elluding her all last week. But Geometry just didn't seem to matter. Cindy couldn't help remembering how miserable she'd been a few months back. She had canceled plans to attend a formal dance with Grant to go whale watching. Actually, she hadn't wanted to watch whales as much as she wanted to avoid having to wear a long formal gown. At the time, she had thought she wanted the freedom to do what she wanted. Instead of feeling free, she found she was lonely without Grant. Now she was heading back down the same path, and she certainly didn't want to go through that again.

Ashley hung the dishtowel over the rack. "Now that you have your homework under control, why not do the same thing with Grant?"

"What do you mean?"

"Well, if he was my boyfriend and we were

having problems, I'd get them straightened out. Even if I had to apologize to do it."

Cindy glanced at the clock on the microwave. It was nearly ten. The Corbetts would be home any minute. By the time she got home, it would be too late to call him. It would have to wait until tomorrow.

Except Grant wasn't in school on Wednesday. Cindy called his house before she went to swim practice. Grant's six-year-old sister, Sally, answered the phone.

"Sally, this is Cindy. Is Grant home?"

"He's asleep."

"Don't wake him, then," she said.

"Okay. I won't."

"Is your mother there?"

"No. She went to get some medicine for Grant. He's sick, so I'm answering the phone."

"Okay," Cindy said. "Will you tell Grant I called?"

"Uh-huh."

"And ask him to call me, okay?"

"Okay."

"You won't forget now, will you?"

"No." And that was the last she heard from anyone in the MacPhearson house that day.

Thursday morning Cindy slammed her locker shut and turned around to find Grant leaning against the locker next to hers. "Heard you called me," he said with a grin.

"Yeah. Thanks for calling me back."

"I didn't hear it until breakfast this morning

when I said something about you and Sally said, 'She called you last night.' "

"Really? How are you feeling?"

"Better. You ought to know by now that Sally isn't the best message service. She means well, but if something exciting happens or the ice cream truck goes by or her favorite TV show comes on, it's all over." He smiled. "What did you want?"

"I guess I wanted to tell you I'm ..." Cindy stopped to let a group of noisy kids go by.

"Yeah?"

"I'm sorry about everything I said the other sight on the porch."

"Yeah, well, maybe I overreacted a bit, too. Trent isn't a bad guy. It's just that I know him, and I know the kind of stuff he pulls." They were walking toward Cindy's first-period class.

"Better get a move on, Lewis," Duffy said as he shot by her. "Tardy bell's about to ring."

"Look," Grant said, taking her by the arm. "Can we talk about this at lunch?"

"You know how crazy lunch always get," Cindy reminded him.

"Then we'll go off some place by ourselves. Some place private."

"How about the gym? We can be alone there," Cindy said. He nodded.

"See you there." Cindy went into class feeling better than she had all week. She had just apologized— it hadn't been nearly as bad as she'd expected!

*   *   *

The lunch bell rang, and Cindy looked both ways before slipping around the corner to wait for Grant near the girls' locker room.

"I feel like I'm James Bond with all this sneaking around," Grant said from behind her.

"Well, you wanted privacy. Not too many people come down here at lunch."

"I can see why," Grant said, wrinkling his nose. "Who wants to eat with all this chlorine smell around you?"

"That's just the pool. You get used to it. Here," she said, taking one-half of her sandwich and handing it to him. They went over to the bleachers and spread their lunches out on the bench in front of them.

"Cindy, I want to talk to you about the other night," Grant began. Cindy heard someone open the side door. She put her finger to her lips signaling Grant to be quiet.

"Here you guys are," Ashley said, squinting against the bright sunshine outside.

"I don't believe it," Grant moaned under his breath.

"Shhh," Cindy whispered.

"Hi," Ashley said, climbing over the bleachers toward them. "I won't stay but a minute. I wanted to check this Biology assignment with Cindy before next period. Lucky thing Duffy saw you two duck in here, or I never would have found you."

"Yeah, lucky thing," Grant said sarcastically.

After Ashley's help with Geometry the other night, Cindy couldn't refuse to help in Biology.

However, Ashley's quick question turned into several, and as she finally got up to leave, the bell rang. "I'm sorry," she said. "You guys probably wanted to be alone, and I came in and spoiled it for you."

"No, actually, we like eating in the gym every once in a while because it smells so good in here," Grant said. Cindy elbowed him as she got up.

"It's okay, Ash." Cindy gathered up the wrappers from their lunch. "We'll talk later."

Grant took Cindy's hand and held her back. "I'll see you after school, okay?"

"I have swim practice."

"Then after practice. I'll come by your house tonight." He kissed her briefly before taking off down the hall.

"Looks like you two are working things out," Ashley said. Cindy wanted to strangle her, but she just gave her an unenthusiastic smile instead.

Swim practice seemed to drag on forever. Cindy kept glancing at the clock. "What's up?" Duffy asked, drifting over next to her. They were treading water in an endurance exercise. Cindy found she had better stamina when she concentrated on something, so she had fixed her eyes on the clock. It didn't seem to be moving.

"Not much. I'm suppose to talk to Grant tonight."

"About time the two of you worked out whatever's bugging you."

"We might have worked it out already if you hadn't been so helpful this afternoon."

"What do you mean?"

"You could have told Ashley you didn't know where we were."

"Oh, she found you, huh?"

"Hey, Lewis, you and your friend Duffy have so much energy, why don't you do five laps before you call it a day?" Coach Roscoe barked. He blew the whistle. "Everybody else, hit the showers."

"Thanks a lot, Duf," Cindy fumed as she shoved off and did her laps. She could barely pull her tired body out of the pool.

"You were a lot more consistent when you weren't in love," Coach Roscoe reminded her. Then he smiled. "But I guess we all are. Hit the showers."

Grant came by about seven. They went into the backyard and sat on the porch swing. "It's nice out here tonight," Grant said. For a while they just rocked gently back and forth in the setting sun. "You didn't tell Ashley I was coming over, did you?"

"No. Why?"

"Well, lately she has had a knack for showing up every time we're together. I'd like to have some time alone with you." He tightened his arms around her.

"I don't know what's gotten into me, Cindy," he continued. "I never used to act this way about a girl. I mean, if she wanted space, I was happy to give it to her. But with you, it's different. You're special."

"That's what Trent said." Cindy felt Grant pull away.

"Oh, yeah?"

"He said it was unusual for you to stick with any girl for very long. Does that mean my time is about up?"

"It's time you forgot about what Trent said and listen to me. I plan to hold on to you, Cindy Lewis, for a long, long time."

Chapter 13

*M*ollie shut her locker and swirled around to almost plow down Heather. "You're hard to find," Heather said.

"Well, I'm right here."

"I know. But I've been calling your house for days, and it seems like you're never home. I thought we could do something tomorrow."

"Can't," Mollie said with a shrug. Heather's face dropped. "I'm watching Mrs. Waters's Pekingese."

"All day on Saturday?"

"They're going to San Diego for the day and won't get back until late at night."

"This new business of yours is really interfering with your social life, Mollie."

"You're telling me," Mollie moaned. The main reason she'd started this silly business in the first place was to impress Greg. But she'd been so busy the last two weeks she hadn't even had time to go to the mall, let alone stop by the pet store and see Greg.

Mollie had never dreamed so many people would need someone to take care of their pets. She was walking the Stevenses' husky every other day. Actually, he was walking her. She would always come dragging back to their house, collapse on the lawn furniture, and hope for the strength to get home. The husky would run around the yard barking and ready to go another mile. The money was okay, but the job was too demanding to be much fun.

"Hey, I know," Mollie said. "Why don't you come over to my house tomorrow?"

"Sounds like a blast. You, me, and the Pekingese," Heather said sarcastically.

"It'll be fun. We'll raid the kitchen and rent some movies. It won't be bad at all."

"Well, okay. Maybe we can go to the mall on Sunday then," Heather said.

"Yeah, Let's plan to do that."

Mollie almost skipped down the hall. She finally had something to look forward to this weekend besides dog hair and waking up early on Saturday. She could put the money she'd earn with the forty dollars she already had and buy something great at the mall. But best of all, she could stop by the pet store and see Greg. Maybe he'd finally get around to asking her out.

*   *   *

Saturday morning Mollie was up and dressed by eight. Right on time, Mrs. Waters rang the doorbell. Ginger was wiggling in her arms, trying to get down. Mrs. Waters set her on the floor and handed Mollie her leash. Mollie took a firm grip on the braided nylon rope.

"Now, dear, we'll be back late tonight, and I'll pick her up then. We hate to keep you up, but Ginger doesn't sleep well away from home." She patted her dog on the head, and the little dog wiggled its knotty tail.

Cindy was standing in the kitchen doorway taking all this in. "I've got to hand it to you, Mollie," she said after Mrs. Waters left. "I never thought there were so many nutty people out there. But it looks like this could turn into a pretty profitable business."

"They're not nutty," Mollie said defensively. "They're just devoted. They care about their animals, just like you do." She picked up Ginger and was trying to unhook her leash.

"Yeah, but I don't go around kissing Winston and finding baby-sitters for Smokey and Cinders if I'm going to the beach for the day. Personally, I think they're crazy."

"You're just jealous that you didn't come up with the idea first."

"Not me," Cindy said, putting her hands up and backing out of the kitchen. "I have enough to do without chasing somebody's precious pooch all over the place." Cindy went upstairs to her room, and Mollie set the little dog on the floor.

"Good morning, Mollie," her mother said, coming into the kitchen. "I thought I heard the doorbell. Is that your charge for the day?"

"Yeah. Isn't she cute?" Mollie asked, looking at the adorable little squashed face and furry tail.

"She is, but you still should try to keep her in your room. Remember our deal."

"Okay." Mollie sighed. She scooped the little dog up in her arms and took it upstairs. She set it on her bed and went into the hall to call Heather. "Are you still coming over?"

"You bet," Heather said. "I'll be over around twelve, if that's okay."

"Sure. Come over any time."

After they hung up, Mollie spent a very boring morning in her room. At first she had fun brushing the Pekingese, but after a while both Mollie and the dog got tired of it. She turned on the radio and started picking up some of the things on her floor, but she was actually doing more dancing than cleaning.

The doorbell rang about twelve-fifteen. "I'll get it," Mollie called. She might as well have saved her breath. It didn't sound like anyone else was home. She opened the door to let Heather in.

They heard a noise on the stairs, and Ginger came bounding down. She ran right by both girls and skidded around the corner into the kitchen. At that point, Winston's loud barking got both girls' attention. Mollie jumped up and noticed the door to the garage wasn't latched. Ginger wasn't in the kitchen anymore. Mollie pushed open the screen door and saw Winston hopping around the barking indignantly as he watched Ginger gobbling up his dog food.

"How'd she get out here?" Heather asked.

"Cindy must have left door open when she left, and Ginger ran through it, I guess." Mollie went toward the dog, who looked up at her and snarled. Mollie took another step toward the dog, and she began to growl.

Mollie backed up. "Okay, have it your way."

"Aren't you going to do something?" Heather asked.

"Like what? Let her bite me? No. I think I'll just let her finish eating first. I know better than to disturb a dog that's eating."

Finally the tiny dog backed away from the empty bowl and Winston closed in on it. He sniffed it and then looked at Mollie with forlorn eyes as if to say, "Did you see that?"

The Peke backed into the corner and began making hacking sounds. "Mollie!" Heather cried. "What's happening?"

"Oh, my gosh," Mollie said in alarm. "Maybe she ate so much she's dying!" At that moment Ginger gave a violent heave and began throwing up Winston's dog food all over the garage.

"Oh, gross," Heather said. "What a mess!"

"You're telling me? We've got to get this cleaned up before my mother gets back. Here," Mollie said, grabbing the dog. "hold her while I get something to clean this up with."

Mollie ran into the house to get some paper

towels. Winston followed her and watched everything she did.

"I know you're hungry, boy, but I've got to take care of this first. Then I'll feed you. I promise." She heard the high-pitched bark of Ginger, and saw a streak shoot by. Winston was gone in a flash. Heather came tearing into the kitchen.

"I lost her," she puffed.

"What do you mean, you lost her?" Mollie wailed. "How could you lose her?"

"Well, she started acting funny, and I thought she was going to barf again, so I put her down. Then she saw one of the cats go by, and she took off."

Mollie heard a loud crash from the living room. Both girls dashed out of the kitchen. Winston was half-buried beneath the end table. All that was visible was his ample hind quarters with a big black tail swinging side to side. Huddled somewhere under the table was a very terrified Ginger. On the floor next to Winston was her mother's crystal unicorn.

"Oh, no," Mollie wailed. She knelt down and picked up the pieces of broken crystal.

"This is my mother's favorite piece of her whole collection. She's going to kill me for this."

"No, she won't," Heather said firmly. "Not if you don't tell her about it. Just hide this someplace and buy her another one."

"But that will take all the money I've got," Mollie protested. Tears filled her big blue eyes and spilled down her face. "Well, it's either that or tell her the truth," Heather said.

"I'd better clean it up before she gets home," Mollie sighed. There would be no new outfits this month. Mollie wiped her eyes and then took hold of Winston's tail. She gave it a tug. "You dumb dog! If you weren't so big, none of this would have happened."

Winston whined and laid his head on Mollie's leg, as if to say, "I'm sorry." Mollie took him by the collar and put him back in the garage. Then she came back, took the broken pieces of the crystal figurine, and put them in a paper towel. She carefully buried that in the garbage.

Mollie heard the back door open, and she spun around to face her mother. With one glance at Mollie's guilty face, Mrs. Lewis asked, "Mollie, what is that mess on the garage floor?"

"Ginger sort of got sick, and I was just going to clean it up." Mollie shot past her mother and went into the garage. All the time she was working, her heart was racing. What if her mother noticed the missing unicorn? She soon found out the answer.

"Mollie Lewis! Come here," her mother said with that unmistakable "you've had it now" tone in her voice. She was holding the paper towel in her hand. "What is this?"

"Broken glass, I guess."

"And I guess it used to be a crystal unicorn."

"I think it is."

"Maybe you'd better tell me why it looks like this," her mother said sternly.

In a flood of tears, Mollie gushed out the whole story and ended with, "I'll buy you another one, I promise."

"Yes, you will. If you hadn't been quite so sneaky about it, you might not have had to," her mother said. "I can't believe you tried to hide this from me, Mollie. What's gotten into you?"

"I don't know," she said miserably.

"I think this dog-sitting business is getting out of hand. It was a good idea, but I think it's time you find yourself another career. By the time you pay for the damages, this one isn't going to be very profitable."

"I sort of figured that out." Mollie sniffed. By the time she replaced the unicorn, she'd be lucky if she had enough money left over to buy a soda. Oh, well, at least there was one good thing to come out of all this. Now she had a good excuse to make a trip to the mall.

Mollie clutched her purse tightly. It had fifty-five dollars in it—everything she had earned dog-sitting, tucked away inside. The first thing she had to do was go to Wexler's Jewelry Store and get her mother another crystal unicorn.

The lady behind the counter carefully fit the crystal figurine into the foam padding and slid it into the gray box. The total came to $52.38. As the saleslady counted out Mollie's change, she said, "Your mother's bound to enjoy that. It's one of our most beautiful pieces."

"I think so, too," Mollie said.

"Just be careful," the clerk warned. "They're very fragile."

"Believe me, I know," Mollie answered, walking out of the store.

"Well, the pet store is just above us on the next level," Heather said.

"I know," Mollie said, this time with much more enthusiasm. They quickly climbed the stairs, not wanting to walk all the way to the center of the mall where the escalators were. Mollie ducked into the pet store and looked around. Greg wasn't there again. Maybe he didn't work on Sundays. She'd never thought about that.

"He's probably just on break again," Heather said.

"You're right," Mollie agreed. The same saleslady came out of the back room.

"Can I help you, girls?" she asked.

"We're looking for Greg," Mollie said.

"I'm sorry. Greg doesn't work here anymore."

"He doesn't?" Mollie said in disbelief. Her heart dove to the pit of her stomach.

"He was offered a job as a veterinary assistant. Yesterday was his last day here. But if there's anything I can do to help you ..."

"No, thanks, anyway." Mollie started out of the pet store. The bag in her hand was a reminder of yesterday's expensive fiasco. Not only had her disastrous day with Ginger cost her all the money she'd made in two weeks, but it also made her miss a last chance to see Greg.

Chapter 14

*O*n Monday morning Mollie came around the corner and saw Grant's tall body looming above some girl. He gestured wildly as he talked. Mollie came up behind him and stopped when she heard the girl say, "Why don't you come over after school and I'll help you." Mollie knew that voice! It was Ashley Corbett.

Grant said, "That would be great. I'll meet you here after school and give you a lift to your house."

"Okay," Ashley replied. Mollie didn't know what she should do. She couldn't stand back and let Ashley move in on her sister's boyfriend. Poor Cindy was just too trusting. She would never do anything to know how to stop Ashley.

Grant stepped aside and went on down the hall without so much as a backward glance. Mollie found herself face-to-face with Ashley. "Oh, hi," Ahsley said. Her face slowly began to redden. "You just missed Grant." She looked back over her shoulder to where he had disappeared among the kids.

"I know," Mollie said icily.

"It's not what you think," Ashley said. "Grant's applying to be the sports editor on the yearbook staff. I used to be an editor for my old school's paper, so I offered to help him."

"Oh."

"Well, look, I'd better get going or I'll be late. And by the way, don't tell Cindy about this. Grant wants to surprise her, okay?" Mollie looked at Ashley skeptically. "Come on, Mollie, it's important."

"Well, okay," Mollie said reluctantly. But why did she believe there was more to it than that? Ashley wanting to help Grant was okay. But why did it have to be at her house and secret from Cindy?

Mollie came home from school that afternoon and found Nicole in the bathroom trying new hairstyles. She pulled her hair away from her face and draped it dramatically over one eye. She looked into the mirror and saw Mollie standing in the doorway behind her. "What's wrong?" she asked, pulling all her hair onto a pile at the top of her head.

Molly took a deep breath and then burst out with, "If you thought you knew something that might hurt someone, would you tell them if you weren't sure, and it turned out that you might be wrong, and the person would get all upset for no reason?"

Nicole let go of her hair and it tumbled down around her face. She turned to face her younger sister. "Mollie, what are you talking about?"

"Well, I saw Ashley and Grant together in the hall today."

"So what? I've seen them in the hall before. So has everyone else at Vista."

"But they were making plans to go to Ashley's after school." Nicole didn't say anything. "Without Cindy," she said emphatically. "You know Cindy has swim practice until five-thirty or six o'clock every day."

Nicole suddenly became more interested in what Mollie was saying. "Are you sure? Maybe you misunderstood what they said."

"Oh, there's no mistake. I talked to Ashley after Grant left, and she said she's helping him with his article for the yearbook application." Mollie rolled her eyes dramatically. "Likely story, huh?"

"Well, maybe she is."

"At her house? And another thing, she said not to tell Cindy anything about it. Doesn't that sound pretty fishy to you?"

"Well, maybe we should wait a couple days, at least until they decide on the yearbook staff. Grant will probably tell Cindy himself."

"I don't know," Mollie said, none too sure that her older sister was giving her the best possible advice.

"You know, Cindy," Nicole continued. "She'll either blow it off and figure it's nothing to worry about. Or she'll get mad and stop talking to Grant. If we're wrong, we might end up causing a fight over nothing."

"Well, maybe you're right. They're supposed to announce the new staff on Friday. I guess we can wait that long." Mollie went down the hall to her room. She still had a feeling that she should tell Cindy what she had seen. After all, Cindy wasn't very smart when it came to romance. In fact, if it hadn't been for Nicole and Mollie, she and Grant might never have gotten together in the first place. Mollie hoped keeping her mouth shut was the right thing to do.

Just before dinner, Mollie was sitting at the snack bar in the kitchen worrying about whether she was doing the right thing. "Mollie, set this on the table," her mother said, handing her the green beans. "Careful, the bottom is hot."

As she set the bowl on the table, a car pulled up. Mollie saw Grant's car in the driveway. Cindy got out and waved to him as he backed out. She came in and tossed her gym bag on the floor near the entry table.

"Hi, shrimp," she said. "What's the matter with you? You look funny. Well, funnier than usual, I mean."

"Grant picked you up from practice?" Mollie asked with relief.

"Yeah. So what?" Nicole walked into the kitchen.

"Grant brought her home," Mollie told Nicole.

"He did? That's great," Nicole answered.

"What's so great about it?" Cindy asked. "What's going on here?"

"Oh, nothing," Mollie said.

"Nothing," Nicole agreed.

"Nothing, except the two of you are strange." Cindy left the kitchen shaking her head.

Nicole turned to Mollie. "See? I told you there was nothing to worry about."

Cindy got out of swim practice early Wednesday afternoon. She came into the kitchen and heard her dad yell, "Yeow!" He plopped a coffee mug onto the counter.

"Hot?" Cindy asked.

"You'd think I'd learn. I've been burning my mouth on this stuff for more than twenty years, but I still haven't learned my lesson."

"Don't be so hard on yourself, Dad," Cindy teased. She went to the freezer and got an ice cube, which she dropped into the mug of hot coffee. "Some of us are just slow learners. Why are you home early?"

"I could ask the same thing," he said.

"Coach let us out early, and I decided to go by Ashley's and get some help on my geometry. We've got a quiz tomorrow."

"Does she know you're coming?"

"I tried to call her, but the line was busy."

"How far is it? I can give you a ride?"

"No, that's okay. I feel like riding my bike."

"Be home in time for dinner."

"You bet. That coffee's probably cool enough to drink now," she said with a wink on her way out the door.

Cindy rode her bike into the Corbett driveway and parked it next to Grant's Trans Am. Cindy got off her bike and went up to the front door. As she rang the bell, Cindy had a funny feeling in the pit of her stomach. Why should it bother her that Grant had stopped by to see Ashley? They were all friends. There was nothing wrong with that. Cindy had told him so herself.

Mrs. Corbett opened the door. "Hello, Cindy," she said with her usual enthusiasm. "Come in, dear." She stepped aside and let her by. "The kids are out back by the pool." The way Mrs. Corbett said it made Cindy think maybe Grant wasn't the only one there. Of course! Grant and some of their friends must have been out driving around and they decided to stop by Ashley's. They must have figured she was still at practice, or they'd have called her, too.

Cindy pushed open the patio door and stepped out into the warm sunshine. She heard laughter and splashing water. It sounded like someone had just jumped into the pool.

Cindy heard Ashley shriek, "Grant, no. Don't you dare! It was an accident. Honest!" Laughing and giggling, she came tearing around the corner of the house and nearly collided with Cindy. She stopped and stared at her. "Oh, Cindy! What are you doing here?"

Cindy looked behind Ashley and saw Grant,

soaking wet in his shorts and a polo shirt. "Um, Grant just stopped by to ... well, we're working on a surprise for you."

"Well, I'm surprised," Cindy said, forcing a smile. "You ought to bring a bathing suit next time, Grant."

"Hey, Cindy, I know this looks funny," Grant said. "But I wasn't in the pool." Cindy looked at him incredulously. "I mean, I was in the pool, but that wasn't what I came over for."

"That's your business."

"I wanted this to be a surprise, but I applied to be sports editor on next year's yearbook staff. Ashley's had some journalism experience, and she's helping me write the essay I have to submit."

"Isn't that nice," Cindy said with control. "Well, I'll let you guys get back to work."

"We're almost finished. Stick around and I'll give you a ride home."

"I have my bike. Thanks, anyway." She went back toward the house. "You better go on home and get out of those wet clothes anyhow."

"I'll call you later," Cindy heard him yell as she shut the patio door.

On the way home, Cindy felt tears stinging her eyes. Why should she be upset? Hadn't she been the one to tell Grant that his friendship with a girl wouldn't change a thing between them? And what about Ashley? She was Cindy's friend. She wouldn't try to steal Grant away just because he and Cindy had an argument.

Mrs. Lewis was in the den reading when Cindy

tore through the house. "That you, Cindy?" she called.

"Yeah."

"Wait a minute," her mother said. "Ashley called, and she wants you to call her."

Cindy ran to her room and slammed the door. She wasn't ready to talk to Ashley yet. She had to cool down first. She began grabbing things from the bottom of her closet and throwing them onto the shelves, not caring if they stayed there or bounded back onto the floor. She kept asking herself what she was so angry about. She'd been the one who invited Ashley to go everywhere with them. Maybe Ashley was telling the truth. Maybe she was helping Grant with his essay. But they sure didn't seem to be working when Cindy showed up.

Cindy felt tears slip down her face. She hated this crying routine. Why was it that whenever she got really mad these days she cried? Before she started dating Grant, she never acted like that. Why, a couple of years ago, she would have gone over to Ashley's and punched her out, and that would have been the end of it. Now she ran the other way and cried about it.

"Can I come in?" Mollie asked in a timid voice.

"No," Cindy snapped.

"Sounds like World War Three in here," she said from behind the door. "Is something wrong? Is it Grant?"

"How'd you know?"

"What happened?"

"I went to Ashley's for some help with my

homework, and guess who else was getting private tutoring?"

"Oh, Cindy," Mollie said, coming in and sitting on her bed, "I'm sorry."

Cindy stopped throwing things and looked over at Mollie. "Why should you be sorry?"

"Because I thought something was going on, and I didn't warn you. But Nicole said that if we let it ride, maybe Grant would tell you himself."

"How long has this been going on?"

"I saw them in the hall on Monday and I wanted to tell you about it then, but Nicole thought we should wait." Mollie sniffed. "She was afraid if we told you and it was nothing, you'd get mad. You're always telling me to stop interfering, and that's what I was trying to do." Her bottom lip began to quiver, and there was a fresh flow of tears on her face.

"There's no reason to cry, Mollie. It's not your fault."

"I just didn't know what to do. Every time I try to help, I make things worse."

"It's okay," Cindy gave her a brief hug, which only made Mollie cry harder.

"I'd like to kill Ashley Corbett," Mollie said vehemently.

"It's not your fault," Cindy said. "I told Grant he could spend time with her and I wouldn't care. Now he's making me eat my words." Why, Cindy wondered, was everything so complicated when you were in love?

Chapter 15

*L*ater that night Cindy was lying on her bed. She'd given up on studying Geoemtry. She couldn't think of anything but Grant and Ashley, anyway. Nicole knocked lightly on the door. "Hey, Cindy, phone's for you."

Cindy rolled off her bed and went into the hall. "Hi, Cindy, it's me."

"Hi, Grant. Did you get your story done?" she asked hotly.

"Almost." Grant cleared his throat. "I thought I could come by, and we could go get a soda."

"I have a headache," Cindy said.

"Come on, Cin, don't be this way."

"What way? I told you I have a headache."

"Okay, I'll just come over to your house and see you."

"I don't feel like it tonight. I have to go study now."

"Cindy ..." But Cindy didn't hear anymore. She had already hung up the phone. Why did he have to call? Now she felt anger building all over again. She went into her room and slammed the door. Cindy paced the floor feeling like a caged animal. If she didn't work off her frustration, she was going to erupt like Mt. St. Helens.

She changed into sweats and jogging shoes and ran down the stairs. "I'm going out," she called.

"This late?" her mother said. "It's nearly dark."

"I'll be back in a little while."

"I don't like you going out alone," her mother said.

"I won't be alone. I'll take Winston," she said. "and I'll be back in ten minutes. I just need some air."

"No more than ten minutes," her mother said firmly.

Winston jumped to his feet and followed Cindy out onto the driveway. "Okay, boy," she told him. "You're one fella I can always count on." He wagged his tail in agreement.

When Cindy got back, she felt a little more relaxed. She sat down at her desk to try to study.

"Phone," Mollie said from the doorway.

"Who is it?" Cindy asked.

"Duffy, I think."

Cindy went out in the hall and picked up the phone. "Hello."

"How's things?" Duffy said cheerfully.

"Okay," she said in a guarded voice.

"That's not what I hear."

"From who?"

"Well, Grant stopped by earlier, and he seemed upset. Said you two had another misuderstanding. What's up?"

"Nothing, Duf. Everything's fine."

"If you say so." But he didn't sound convinced.

"I say so. Look, I got to go. I'm plowing through this stupid geometry."

"I thought Ashley was helping you with that."

"Well, she's already helped enough for one day," Cindy said sarcastically, feeling the anger burning again but trying to not to let it show. After she had dragged Ashley along everywhere she went, even on her dates with Grant, she couldn't tell Duffy anything was wrong until she knew for sure it was. Everyone had tried to warn her to be careful: Duffy, Mollie, Carey. And she hadn't listened to any of them. She wasn't up to I-told-you-sos tonight.

"I'll see you at school tomorrow then?" Duffy asked.

"Sure. See you." Cindy hung up and went back to her room.

Thirty minutes later Cindy threw her pencil into the air and screamed, "I'll never learn this stuff!" Geometry had to be the dumbest thing she ever would learn. She could get the right answer, that was easy. But she didn't always use the right theories, so the whole thing might as well have been wrong. Cindy glanced over at the clock on her bedside table. It was only eight-thirty, but she was already exhausted.

"Hey, Cindy," Mollie said, opening the door.

"Don't you ever knock?" Cindy snapped. All the sisterly tenderness from earlier that afternoon was gone.

"Grant's here. He wants to see you."

"Tell him I'm busy," Cindy said, picking up the pencil she'd thrown earlier and turning her back on Mollie. Right now she would rather struggle with geometry than face Grant.

"Tell him yourself," Mollie retorted. "I'm not your maid."

"Oh, all right!" Cindy slammed her book shut and followed Mollie down the stairs. Grant was talking to Nicole when he heard her on the stairs and looked over at her.

"Hi," he said with a smile of relief on his face. "I thought you might not come down."

Cindy knew Nicole and Mollie were listening to everything they said. "Let's go outside," she said and led the way to the back porch.

"I know you said I shouldn't come by," Grant began, "but I was hoping you'd talk to me if I came over."

"I have a quiz tomorrow, and I need to study."

"I won't keep you long."

"Look, Grant, I was in the middle of working a problem when you came. I need to get back to it before I forget what I was doing."

"How long do you plan to keep this up?"

"I don't know what you're talking about."

"I just want to know how long you plan to keep this freeze going. Then I'll know when it's safe to start talking to you again."

"I have to get back inside." Cindy opened the door. "Are you coming?"

"No. I'll just go around the side of the house. Call me if you change your mind. I'll be home."

Cindy was lying on her bed tossing a tennis ball into the air and counting the number of times she could throw it up and catch it without missing. After Grant left, she gave up on studying. Nicole knocked lightly, and Cindy lost her concentration. The tennis ball dropped next to her on the bed. "You busy?" Nicole asked.

"You just made me blow the world record for most consecutive catches of a tennis ball lying down. I was thinking of writing to *Ripley's Believe It or Not.*"

"Try the *Guinness Book of World Records.* They're much more interested in stuff like that. And speaking of interest, how much longer do you think you can keep Grant's interest if you don't talk to him?"

Cindy sat up on the bed as Nicole sat down. "Don't deny it. He was here all of five minutes before you sent him packing. Do you want to hand him to Ashley?"

"No."

"Then do something about it. Maybe he was telling the truth about working on an essay. When Mollie heard them talking in the hall, Ashley told her the same thing they told you. Grant was applying for that yearbook position, and he wanted to surprise you."

"But what if it's more than that? What if Ashley is interested in more than his writing?"

"Then stop making it easy for her."

"You mean talk to Grant?"

"Might help. He obviously cares about you. He called, and he came by. He's made the first move, twice, and it probably wasn't easy for him either time. If you keep slamming doors in his face, eventually he's going to give up and go home. Or worse yet, he might go to Ashley."

"Maybe I'd better talk to him." Cindy sighed.

Nicole got to her feet. "Well, I'll let you get back to that important record setting you were doing when I came in."

"Thanks." Sometimes it was pretty great having Nicole for a sister. Cindy looked at her clock. It was 10:15, too late to call Grant. But tomorrow she was going to straighten out this mess.

Cindy was waiting outside of Grant's fourth-period class. "You're going with me," she said, pulling him by the arm. "And this time we're locking the door behind us."

Cindy led Grant out to the parking lot, and they got into his car. "We could get detention for this, you know?" he said.

"I'm worth it," Cindy said. "I wanted privacy, and this seemed like the best place to get it."

"Okay."

"I did a lot of thinking last night," Cindy said.

This was going to be much harder on a real person. She'd practiced talking to the mirror this morning, and it had been easy. But with Grant sitting there looking at her, it was a lot harder.

"When Trent asked me to write to him, I couldn't understand why you'd be upset. I said a lot of things about friends and how it shouldn't matter if they're male or female. But I'm not so sure I can believe that anymore. Things used to be so simple. If you liked somebody, you went out to play with them at recess whether they were a boy or a girl. But now everything's different."

"I know."

"I mean, when I saw you come tearing around that corner, your hair all dripping wet, and both of you laughing, I was ... I was jealous. I never thought it would bother me if you and Ashley were friends. And it would be okay if I felt about you like I feel about Duffy. If that had been Duffy at Ashley's yesterday, it would have been fine."

Cindy forced herself not to cry. She had swallowed enough pride telling Grant all this, but she positively refused to cry about it.

Grant reached out to her. "Come here," he said as his arms encircled hers. "Do you know how much I've wanted to hear you say that?"

Cindy shook her head.

"I thought you'd never care about me the way I care about you," he said. "Since you told me it was okay to have female friends. I had the feeling that if I walked out of your life tomorrow, you'd never miss me."

"Well, I would," Cindy said, looking into his deep blue eyes.

"It's about time you told me that. Now I want to tell you a few things," he said, settling back into his seat. "Like what I was doing at Ashley's in the first place."

"Grant, you don't have to."

"Yes, I do. Last week I heard the announcement on the P. A. about joining the yearbook. For the first time since I moved here, I felt interested in doing something that was part of the school. Then I went to get the application, and I met Ashley there. She was applying for the job of feature editor. I asked her not to tell you about it because I wanted to surprise you. Anyway, she offered to help me with my essay. She's had more experience than I have because she worked on the school paper at her last school."

"But why didn't you tell me about it?"

"I wanted to surprise you," Grant studied his hands. Without looking at Cindy, he said, "Mostly because I didn't want you to know about it in case I didn't get it."

"But why?"

"Cindy, can't you understand? Sometimes it's tough having a girlfriend who never fails at anything."

"You haven't seen my geometry grades lately," she said.

"I'm serious. You're cute and popular and smart, and you're a great swimmer, and sometimes I feel like I'm just tagging along doing nothing."

"Grant, that's crazy. You could be on the swim team if you wanted to."

"And then we'd be competing again. The swim team is *your* thing, Cindy. I want something of my own. I'm tired of watching everyone else run Vista."

"Then I hope you get the job. How did the article turn out?"

"Okay. I had to turn in a sample layout, too. I've only had a semester of Journalism in Hawaii. I hope it's enough." He sighed.

"I'm sure it is. And just in case ..." Cindy put her arms around him and kissed him. "That's for luck."

"I'll need lots of it."

"No problem. I got more where that came from." She kissed him again.

They walked into the school hand in hand. Cindy didn't even mind that she missed lunch. This coversation was much more important. She had decided that she would apologize to Ashley for jumping to conclusions. After all, Ashley was only helping Grant out as a good friend would.

Coming out of sixth period, Cindy glanced at her watch. If she hurried, she would catch Ashley before practice. "You on your way to the gym?" Duffy asked as he ran to catch up to her.

"Not yet. I've got to find Ashley first."

"How come?"

"I need to straighten something out," she said.

"I'll go with you," Duffy said, falling easily into step beside her.

"Thanks, but I need to do this alone. I'll meet you at the gym."

"Okay." He turned and went down the corridor to the gym. Cindy knew where Ashley would be. The new yearbook staff list was being posted after school outside the journalism room. She would bet that's where she was going to find both Ashley and Grant.

She saw Grant first. He was reading the list of names. Suddenly he jumped up and punched the air. "Yeah!" he shouted.

Cindy tried to push her way to him. He had gotten the editor's job. She was sure of it. But instead of breaking out of the crowd and rushing to her, he spun around and grabbed Ashley by the waist and lifted her high into the air. "We did it!" he yelled.

Ashley laughed and threw her arms around his neck. "Oh, Grant, I'm so proud of you. We'll have so much fun together on the yearbook. It's going to be great!" She put her hands on either side of his face and kissed him. Really kissed him. Cindy didn't know if Grant's look of surprise was because of the kiss or because he saw Cindy standing on the fringe of the crowd. She didn't want to find out. Her cheeks flaming, she turned and ran blindly down the hall.

"Cindy, wait!" Grant yelled. But she had a good head start on him even though he was faster. Cindy ducked into the girls' locker room before he could stop her. He pounded on the door, yell-ing. "Cindy, if you don't get out here, I'm coming in!"

"Let him," she said, tears blinding her vision. She went out of the back door into the pool area and crashed into Duffy.

"Hey, what's wrong?"

"Everything," Cindy said. And for the first time in all the years they'd been friends, Cindy cried in Duffy's arms.

Chapter 16

*A*ll day Friday, Cindy managed to avoid Grant. She dodged his phone calls and ducked out of sight whenever she saw him in the halls. All of Nicole's advice had been fine the first time, but she wasn't going to let Grant have another chance to tromp on her feelings. It had taken a lot for her to tell Grant how she felt. And then even after she explained everything to him, he had grabbed Ashley and hugged her. He'd made it pretty clear Cindy's feelings didn't matter.

There wasn't any swim practice on Friday afternoon, but Cindy went down to the gym and swam a few laps anyway. She came out of the school about four-thirty. The parking lot was deserted. Cindy unlocked her bike and backed it out. She hopped on and began pedaling toward home. Grant's red car pulled in close to her and the window slid down. "Can we talk?" he said. He was steering the car and trying to watch the road and Cindy at the same time.

"What about?" She didn't let up her pace.

"You know what about," he said irritably.

"There's nothing to discuss." She gave a burst of energy and pulled out ahead of him. Grant gunned the motor and drove about a half a block in front of her and jumped out of the car. He grabbed the handlebars as she tried to ride past him. She put her feet abruptly on the ground to keep from falling over.

"What do you want, Grant?"

"I know what you saw yesterday. But it wasn't what it looked like. I didn't even know you were standing there."

"Would it have made any difference?"

"Well, would it have made any difference if I'd been in San Simeon with you?" he snapped.

"What are you talking about?"

"Ashley told me about those two guys from San Diego you met in San Simeon."

"What about them?"

"Don't play dumb, Cindy. You lay a guilt trip on me, and then I find out you were having a great time in San Simeon watching movies in some guy's hotel room. How can you be mad at me for one innocent kiss?"

Cindy felt the heat rising in her face. She had been such a fool. How could Ashley say something like that? Cindy was usually a good judge of character, but Ashley had completely fooled her.

"Well, are you going to deny it?"

"There's nothing to deny. We did meet two guys in San Simeon. But I suppose Ashley neglected to tell you that I went back to the hotel room and took a nap while she entertained them. Then we sat on the floor and watched a rerun of *St. Elmo's Fire*. That was the extent of the whole stimulating weekend."

"Well, you could have told me."

"Why? There was nothing to tell. I had no reason to feel guilty. *I* didn't kiss anyone," she said pointedly.

"I didn't kiss *her*. She kissed me."

"Well, I hope you enjoyed it. Now if you'll excuse me," she said with a violent jerk on the handlebars of her bike. "I have to go home." She pedaled off furiously, the heat of her anger helping her to set a new world's record for speed cycling.

Duffy called early Saturday morning. "I'm coming by to get you in thirty minutes, and I don't want any arguments. We're going to the beach. There's some great waves out there just going to waste."

"Oh, Duf." Cindy sighed. She knew what he was up to. She was grateful he hadn't mentioned the incident at the pool. What a great friend. No judgments or I-told-you-so, just listening and understanding. He hadn't even tried to defend Grant for a change. It was a good thing, too. The way Cindy felt Thursday afternoon, she would have thrown Duffy in the pool if he'd tried.

"I won't take no for an answer, Lewis. I'll be there in half an hour. Be ready."

Cindy barely had time to run upstairs and change and put a few snacks into a basket before she heard Duffy's car out front. She grabbed her stuff and went out to the car. She was glad Duffy had called her.

They went by Carey's house and picked her up. She smiled when she saw Cindy. "It's great to see you again. I haven't seen much of you lately. I haven't seen much of Ashley either." Cindy shrugged her shoulders indifferently, and Duffy nudged Carey's leg and gave her his change-the-subject look.

They found a good spot and set out their towels and blankets. Everyone was showing up, and it was inevitable that Grant would, too. He got out of his car and lifted his board easily above his head as he came confidently down the beach.

Cindy was determined not to let him put a damper on this beautiful day. She, Anna, and Carey went down into the water and dove into incoming waves. Cindy ducked into a wave and then surfaced and rolled onto her back. She let it carry her back to shore. She rolled over to her knees and stood up just in time to see Ashley coming toward them. Cindy couldn't believe the nerve of her. How could she walk up like everything was the same?

Her life had been so perfect until Ashley came into it. She'd gone out on a limb to make Ashley feel welcome in Santa Barbara. The only thanks she got was Ashley stealing Grant away from her with a pack of vicious lies.

Cindy strode out of the water and picked up her board. "Cindy? Are you okay?" Anna called.

"I need some room to breathe," Cindy said. She got onto her board and started paddling out toward the open sea. She needed a place to think for a while.

Cindy sat on her board and felt the gentle rocking motion of the waves. Every once in a while, one would lift her high into the air so she could see clearly everyone on the shore. Cindy lay back on her board, her legs dangling in the water, and looked at the sky overhead.

The wind was picking up, and the waves were getting rougher. Cindy sat up and decided she had gone far enough, and it was time to go back. She saw a small figure enter the water carrying a surfboard. From this far out, it was impossible to tell who it was. She thought he or she might be coming out for her. Everyone probably thought she was doing something stupid. She had decided to turn back and save whoever it was a long trip out.

Cindy turned on her board and got to her knees. Gracefully, she rose to her feet and began riding the swells into shore. As she studied the figure coming toward her, she saw it was a girl. Then she recognized the black-and-white suit she knew was Ashley's.

What had gotten into her? What was wrong with everyone else? Ashley shouldn't be in the surf. It was too rough for an inexperienced surfer today. Cindy decided on top of everything else, Ashley was pretty stupid. If she was trying to impress Grant, there were safer ways to do it. Cindy continued working her way back toward shore. She hoped Ashley would be smart enough to turn back, too.

Ashley was about fifty feet in front of Cindy when Cindy shouted, "Go back! It's too rough."

Ashley turned around on the board, and Cindy was relieved she had heard her at all. Cindy couldn't believe it when she saw Ashley get to her knees and then try to stand up. She should have stayed on her stomach. There was no way Ashley could handle these waves. It was taking all of Cindy's skill to stay up.

Cindy saw the wave flip Ashley, sending the board high into the air. It popped to the surface again, but Ashley didn't come up with it. Cindy dropped off the board and swam back toward Ashley's board. It was rough swimming against the powerful waves, and she didn't see any sign of Ashley.

Then Ashley's panic-stricken face bobbed to the surface sputtering and gasping for air. "Hold on," Cindy yelled above the waves.

Cindy managed to grab Ashley's surfboard. She struggled to climb on. The waves kept slapping her back into the swirling sea. With a burst of strength, Cindy pulled herself onto the board and held on while it bobbed and shook. She steadied herself on the board, then began pulling it through the water toward Ashley, whose terrified face bobbed up and down just ahead of her. Twice Cindy reached for Ashley's outstretched hand and missed. There wasn't much time left.

Nearly hysterical, Cindy made one final grab and managed to grab Ashley's arm. She pulled Ashley onto the board and started paddling them both back to shore.

Chapter 17

As they got closer to shore, Cindy could hear Ashley crying above the crash of the water. Cindy's board had already washed ashore. Anna and Carey were pulling it out of the water. Grant and Duffy started out to meet Cindy and Ashley. When Cindy got close to shore, she bailed off the board and let the others take Ashley on in.

Cindy collapsed onto her towel and shook all over. She wasn't sure if it was from fear or anger. Ashley had nearly drowned. If Cindy hadn't been near her, no one could have gotten to her in time. She shuddered at the thought of it.

Ashley dropped onto the towel next to her. Cindy looked over at her. "I can't believe you did that," Ashley said softly.

"What did you want me to do? Keep going and let you drown?" Cindy asked coldy.

"I wouldn't have known what to do," Ashley said.

"Well, you're lucky I did, because that was a stupid thing to do. But now you can go on back to Grant. But stay out of the water for the rest of the afternoon. I'm too tired to pull you out again."

"Cindy, I'm sorry," Ashley said. Then she began to cry. "I never wanted to hurt you." She sniffed. "It's just that you have everything. You've got the greatest family and all these friends, and on top of everything else, you have Grant, too. It's just not fair."

"I'll tell you what's not fair," Cindy said with rising anger. "I liked you. I put my friendships on the line for you. I trusted you. I never thought you'd stab me in the back like you did."

"That was wrong. I know. But do you know what I would give to be even a little bit like you? Every day you go home to a family that's just like *The Cosby Show,* and I go back home to a microwave dinner and my mother."

"Is that my fault?"

"No, but it's not just your family. When I walk down the halls alone, no one sees me. But when I'm with you, everyone says hi. I wanted to be like you, and ended up destroying the best thing I had. Your friendship."

Ashley bent her face into her knees and rocked gently back and forth as she cried. Everyone else had drifted off down the beach, but Cindy was sure that their angry voices had carried enough for the rest of them to know what had been said.

"Ashley, look. You don't have to be like me. You're a neat person just the way you are."

"I've been so stupid, Cindy. How can you be nice to me? I wouldn't blame you if you never spoke to me again."

"Everyone deserves a second chance, Ash."

"I wasn't trying to steal Grant away from you. I only wanted to help him with his essay," she said sincerely. "That afternoon when you came over to the house, it was nothing. Then when I saw how upset you were, I knew I'd lost your friend-ship, and I didn't think it mattered anymore. Now I know better. No guy is worth losing your best friend over."

Cindy felt a jab in her stomach. Poor Ashley had no one else. Cindy was her best friend, and she had lost faith in her and deserted her.

"But no friend is worth losing a guy like Grant either." Ashley looked at her through teary eyes. "You better get over there and straighten things out before some sneaky girl like me really does try to take him away."

Cindy got up and went over to the rest of the kids. "Hey, Duf, start the fire for the hamburgers, why don't you?" Cindy said. "I'll bet I'm not the only hungry one after all the excitement of this morning!"

She went over to Grant. "Can I talk to you?" she asked. He nodded, and they turned away from the others and started up the beach.

"That was some rescue," Grant said.

"It was nothing," Cindy said modestly. "I had to

pull her from the water, or I'd always wonder if you came back to me because she wasn't around anymore.'

"You're sick." Grant laughed. "But seriously, I never left you. You were the one who wouldn't talk to me."

"Still mad about the weekend in San Simeon?" she asked.

"No. You still mad about that kiss the other day?"

"No."

"You know," he said, putting his arm around her, "I was thinking about our schedules for next year."

"What?" She laughed.

"Well, the other day I was in the counselor's office changing my schedule to add yearbook staff, and I got to looking over some of the electives we have at Vista. There's one course I think would be particularly helpful for us."

"Oh yeah? What's that?"

"Creative Communication." He laughed. "If we would just start talking about things that bother us, we'd have a lot less fights."

"Did you sign up for it?"

"Well, then I didn't have a reason to. But if you put your name on the list, I'll try to get the seat behind you."

"You're on." He took her hand again, and they began to walk along the water. It splashed their feet as they walked. Cindy stopped and rested her head against Grant's strong shoulder. They looked out at the ocean. The clear sky was clouding over, and it looked like a storm might be blowing in. But that was okay. With Grant to lean on, she could weather any storm.

Here's a look at what's ahead in TOO MANY COOKS, the ninth book in Fawcett's "Sisters" series for GIRLS ONLY.

"Don't worry, Mrs. Field," Nicole said firmly. "We have everything under control. If you'll just show us where to set up the buffet table, we can get started."

"Of course." The woman fluttered her hands in a nervous gesture that made Nicole wish for extra patience. "I think we're going to be in the director's room, no, or was that—"

The girls waited impatiently. Mrs. Field called to a tall young man who was standing with his back to her.

"Rob! Where do we want the food set up?"

"In the large meeting room, Mrs. Field. We agreed on it yesterday," the young man answered calmly. He walked toward them and directed a friendly smile toward all three girls.

Nicole, attracted by his good-natured expression, smiled back. "If you'll just show us the way—"

"Certainly. Can I give you a hand?"

Cindy shook her head. "I'm fine."

With a quiet efficiency that came as a welcome relief after the vice-president's dithering, he ushered them into a long room, pointed out two tables set up for their use, then introduced himself.

"I'm Rob O'Neal. I work her part-time as sort of an all-around gofer when I'm not in class at UCSB."

"Really?" Nicole, intrigued by the humor in his intelligent hazel eyes, felt a rush of instantaneous pleasure that she hadn't experienced in months. Steady, *idiot,* she told herself silently. You're too old to have a crush.

Whether she was too old or not, the tall young man with his broad shoulders and dark wavy hair certainly made her pulse quicken. And she noticed, holding back a frown, that he'd made an impression on Mollie, too. She was gazing up at him with wide eyes.

"Mollie," she said, more sharply than she intended, "go back and get the tablecloths, please."

Mollie blinked at her sister in surprise. "You're holding them," she pointed out.

"Oh, of course," Nicole murmured, feeling incredibly foolish.

But Rob didn't seem to notice. He was helping Cindy lift the heavy hamper onto the table with such easy charm that she didn't even bristle.

Nicole hurried to lay out the white linen, then put Mollie to work unloading the food. She picked up a large jug and turned to Rob.

"Can you show me where to get some water to mix the punch?"

"Sure." He led the way to a water cooler, and Nicole, her usual poise a little shaky, asked shyly, "What are you studying?"

Rob smiled at her. "Don't laugh. I'm majoring in art history."

"Mais non!" Nicole hurried to assure him. "I wouldn't laugh. I think that's marvelous. I'm interested in art history myself. Why should I laugh?"

"Some of my friends don't think the subject macho enough," Rob said with a grin.

Nicole, covertly inspecting his broad shoulders and firm, athletic build, thought to herself that *macho* was an immensely inadequate term to apply to such an intelligent, personable guy.

"Careful," Rob said, his hazel eyes twinkling.

With a start, Nicole realized that her jug was about to overflow. She gave herself a mental shake even as she smiled up at the young man.

"Thanks. I'd better get the punch made."

"If I can do anything else, just yell," Rob offered, adding, "I hope you can spare some time away from the buffet. There are some nice paintings here, aside from the special sculpture exhibit. It would be a shame to miss them while you're here. I'll show you my favorites."

"I'd like that." Nicole's smile deepened, and the glow in her soft blue eyes made Rob linger another moment.

TAF-68